MASQUERADE

LISA MARIE RICE

OLIVERHEBERBOOKS

PUBLISHER'S NOTE: This is a work of fiction. Names, characters, places, and incidents either are the product of the author's imagination or are used fictitiously. Any resemblance to actual persons, living or dead, business establishments, events, or locales is entirely coincidental.

Published by Oliver-Heber Books

Masquerade ©2018 by Elizabeth Jennings

0 9 8 7 6 5 4 3 2 1

1

BOSTON

TEN YEARS AGO

Calvin Burns stroked the beautiful back of the woman he loved, Anya Voronova. It was snowing outside his miserable, shabby dump of a studio apartment, the white mantle covering the overfilled dumpsters, filling in the cracks in the sidewalk, softening the smell of rot and mold.

But inside his room was magic. He didn't see the sagging bed, plyboard desk, scratched appliances. With Anya in the room, it was like being in a palace housing the rarest of treasures. Her naked body on his cheap rumpled bed glowed like the finest ivory. Her long blonde hair rippled down her back, gleaming gold.

Fuck, *listen to him.*

Cal was an engineer. Engineers were bound by facts and equations and hard cold math. If his profs or students in the post grad engineering classes he taught could read his mind right now, they'd freak. Cal Burns did math. Cal Burns didn't do poetic.

But then, nobody else had Anya Voronova as a lover. She'd inspire a gorilla to poetry. She was like winning the lottery and discovering the cure for cancer and inventing computers all wrapped up in one winning package.

He tapped out *We are the Champions* on her satiny back, right above the dimple over her perfect ass.

"Mmm." She made a throaty sound of pleasure.

"Like that, do you?" Cal asked. He didn't have to ask. Anya always made her pleasure — and displeasure — known. She didn't play games. He loved that about her.

But then, he loved everything about her.

She smiled at him over her shoulder, light blue eyes gleaming. "Do you know who used to do that?"

Cal froze. "Do what?" Was she going to talk about some lover she'd had before him who'd touched that perfect back? Jealousy shot through him in a spurt of bile.

"Tapping something rhythmic on the back of a woman. Goethe did that, tapping out the hexameters of one of his poems on his lover's back. In his palazzo in Rome."

Goethe. Cal had only discovered who Goethe was since he'd started dating Anya and the first time he saw the name written he would have pronounced it Go-thee. Luckily she pronounced it out loud first. Ghew-tay.

And fuck if he knew what a hexameter was.

Another thing about this beautiful woman. She was cultivated as hell, knew everything there was to know about non-scientific, non-engineering things. Cal more or less had the scientific, engineering side of things down pat, so together they were going to rule the world.

"Well." Cal sighed, smoothing the palm of his hand over the satiny skin of Anya's lower back. "Not a poet. Couldn't write a poem to save my life."

She chuckled and slowly turned over. Every time Cal met those bright summer-sky blue eyes, it was like a punch to the stomach. She was so beautiful she took his breath away.

He hadn't moved his hand but her turning over placed his hand on her stomach. It wasn't a hardship. That very soft skin covered sleek firm muscles all over. She smiled right into his eyes, placing her hand over his, pushing it down.

"I don't know, darling," she whispered. "In some things you're an artist."

And she moved her long slim legs apart and the hard punch of lust nearly brought him to his knees. She smiled. She knew exactly what she did to him.

One leg bent, one long leg open to the side and there she was — open to him. They'd made love not long ago and she was still pink and swollen there. Glistening from her juices. Cal remembered vividly shaking as he came and jetted what felt like half his bodily fluids into the condom and feeling how wet she was when he pulled out.

Her sex was a living embodiment of their love-making, like she'd been branded. He liked that, liked the thought of her being branded by him. Her sex, her breasts ... the nipples were still hard and deep pink from his mouth. There was a little whisker burn on the ivory skin of her breasts which he'd feel sorry for if he hadn't loved sucking on her nipples so much. She hadn't complained.

In a deeper way, he was branded, too. Highly sexed by nature, Cal now thought of sex exclusively in terms of Anya. No one else turned him on at all. He couldn't even consider having another woman, not when he had the most beautiful woman in the world in his bed, who was also whip smart and understood him.

And loved him.

That was the real kicker. She loved him.

"Cal," she breathed, and all the hairs on his body stood up. He was already hard as a rock. He was always semi-aroused when around her. But when they were naked together, his dick simply wouldn't go down.

"Honey." There was a slight question in the word. What did she want? Whatever she wanted, he'd give to her. He'd give her the moon if he could.

Her huge, bright blue eyes locked onto his face. "Touch me."

Cal shuddered. God, yes. He reached out and gently pushed her legs further apart. The skin of her inner thighs felt warm and incredibly soft against the skin of his palm. His hands were big and rough. He'd been into martial arts since he was a kid and had had a karate period. He had tough, calloused hands. But he knew from experience that no matter how rough his hands were, they didn't scratch her skin. He knew exactly how to touch her, where and how hard.

"That's it," Anya whispered as his hand rose along her thigh, higher and higher.

Cal sat on the side of the bed and just looked at her, stretched out before him like a feast, legs apart, eyes heavy.

There was some painter from some time in the past who'd painted this painting ... he didn't remember the name of the artist, or the style or the name of the painting. That wasn't in his wheelhouse, though it was in hers. She was the one who'd showed him the image in a book.

All he remembered was skin that glowed like pearls on the canvas, the woman looking straight at the viewer, long blonde hair covering part of her body, one hand on her belly. It was a famous painting and if his mind hadn't been blasted by lust maybe he'd remember what it was called, but he did remember the beauty of the model that seared the eyes.

That was what Anya looked like, only she was more slender and her hair was honey blonde not red. But other than that, she was eternal woman.

Cal shifted his eyes to her belly, where his hand lay next to hers. Just the sight of their hands together was erotic, let alone how she was posed. His hands were big and callused from years at the dojo. He could shatter four bricks with the edge of his hand but here it looked out of place against her delicate skin. Her hand was slender and pale, the hand of an artist. Male and female.

He slid his hand further down and covered her mound, like a flesh-colored bikini bottom. She had a cloud of ash-brown hair covering her sex, it was so soft to the touch it felt like a cloud too. Small dots of her juices were threaded through her pubic hair like tiny pearls.

She smiled at him, meeting his eyes, then hers travelled over his body down to his groin, where he was as hard as a club. He felt more blood rush to his dick. It was almost painful.

She smiled up into his eyes. "Just from looking at you?"

"Just you breathing does the trick, princess."

She rolled her eyes, as she always did when he called her princess. But the fact was, she *was* a princess, sort of. Her asshole father, who was insanely rich, never failed to mention in interviews that he was descended from Russian royalty. His great-great- a billion times great-grandfather had been a cousin of the czar a million years ago when Russia had czars. It was in every interview with the man. Anya never mentioned it but her father did. Often.

He was a dickhead. Cal hated him and he hated Cal right back.

Not that Cal cared. Not when he had his princess looking at him with heat in her glowing blue eyes.

She lifted her leg and placed her foot right over his dick. Cal closed his eyes because it was just too much stimulation. Her foot was beautiful too, slender, pretty, with blue toenail polish. She rubbed it up and down him and his breathing went ragged.

He had to do something to even this up.

Cal turned his hand, started stroking her. He heard a sharp intake of breath and opened his eyes to see her closing hers. Fuck yeah. He wasn't alone here. She was wet and pink and slightly swollen, from the last time they'd made love and from her body preparing for the next time.

He watched as his hand stroked her, the wet skin like satin. A finger traced her opening, around and around, lingering at the clitoris. He knew her so well. Her excitement was so fascinating he almost forgot his own.

Around and around ... her thighs trembled.

Yeah, baby.

He slipped his finger inside her, relishing the small cry. She convulsed around his finger sharply and he could see her stomach muscles pull. When his princess came, she came with her whole body.

She wasn't quite there yet, though. Close, but not there.

"Cal ..." Anya whispered.

He leaned down, one hand planted on the bed right next to her pale firm breast. "Sweetheart." He pulled his finger out, slid it back in. She convulsed again, a sharp pull of her sex. Her hands were trembling.

His were, too.

"Come to me," she pleaded and it wasn't in him to deny her. Of course he would come to her. He was born to come to her.

He slid a second finger into her silky warmth, holding her open, placed a knee on the bed and mounted her, sliding into her in the exact moment she started coming.

Oh my god, she was so beautiful when she came. He never got tired of it. He wanted to spend the rest of his life watching her. There was a ring in his pants pocket with a tiny diamond in it. So tiny you could hardly see it, but the promise behind the ring was big. He was hers, forever.

She was arched back, long neck exposed. He lowered his mouth to her neck and as his lips touched her skin, she came even harder, pulsing against his dick. There was an electrical connection that nearly stopped his heart.

He pressed inside her, mouth on her neck, feeling the fluttering of her heart. His own heart was thundering inside his chest, with excitement, with love.

Man, he loved her. He didn't think it was possible to love any human being as much as he loved Anya Voronova, his princess. He felt her skin against his, but it was like her skin had been removed and he could feel her insides, too. Her heart beating, her muscles pulling, her lungs expanding. He was inside her and she was inside him.

It was exhilarating and a little scary too.

But, hell, worth it.

Cal held himself still while she worked her way through her orgasm, hyperaware of everything going on with her. Her sex clenching around his, her arms and legs holding him tightly, the way she arched her back and stopped breathing for a long moment, as she went inside herself, completely in the moment.

Then she crested, a sharp moan coming from her, her hips rotating, almost dancing around his dick while coming. He let her because it was a way for her body to be prepared.

Cal could be rough. He didn't want to be, particularly not with his princess, but it was the way he was wired. The only way it could work was if she came and came hard and was soft and wet afterward. So he gritted his teeth as she climaxed, then came down gently, her entire body lax and mellow. Arms and legs falling back onto the mattress, wet and soft inside.

Now he could let loose.

Cal lowered his entire body onto her and buried his face in the pillow next to hers. In his excitement he didn't want to mark her, even – God forbid! – bite her. In the early days he'd been so worked up he marked that perfect ivory skin a couple of times and it had appalled him.

He slid his hands up her slim legs and lifted them and opened them a little, so that — ah — he reached deep inside her. If he could, he'd have touched her heart with his dick. As it was, he did his best.

And then all thoughts fled his head as he became a male animal with his mate.

He retained just enough control not to pound her, but it was hard. Every single cell in his body registered acute mind-numbing pleasure as he moved in and out of her, fast then faster. She was soft and warm and all his. Skin to skin, heart to heart, on her and in her, he moved, heart pounding, barely registering pleasure when she convulsed and came again. Her arms held him so tightly, but not as tightly as he held her. He wanted to stay inside her forever but when her hands moved to his butt and her fingers curled in and she nipped his earlobe — he lost it.

Cal moved as fast and as hard as he could, feeling her pleasure, feeling that he wasn't hurting her but pleasing her, but it was way too much. Too much stimulation — that soft, creamy skin, that luscious mouth kissing his ear, her soft, wet sex like a glove around him ...

He erupted with a great groan, lungs bellowing because there wasn't enough air in the world to contrast the enormous heat inside him, like a volcano exploding, hips making short fast jabs inside her until it was over and he collapsed on top of her, completely spent.

His breathing gradually slowed down and he gained the use of his body back. Every time it was as if he entered some secret kingdom where he gave her so much power over him he had to work his way back into himself.

He did it this time, too. But this time, there was a reason for him to get back in control of himself. He had big news. Big *big* news. The biggest.

His face was still buried in the pillow next to hers and a huge grin broke out, one he couldn't control. He let it bloom because ... *hot damn.* His life — their lives — were about to change.

It was supposed to be a surprise because it was so big he'd been afraid to blow the possibility of it out of proportion with her. They'd barely talked about it because he didn't want to jinx it and he didn't want to see disappointment in her eyes if he didn't get it.

Already the difference in status between them was huge, an almost unbridgeable gap. But he was an engineer and his love for her had built the bridge between them, which existed only when they were in their little world of two. And here, in his slum of a flat. He'd been to her palatial mansion only once and the memory was so painful he winced every time he thought of it.

She was the daughter of an immensely rich aristocrat and he was the son of a runaway mom and a drunk truck driver of a father, who'd cut off relations when Cal wanted to go to college instead of driving a truck like his dad.

But all of that was going to change. Something big was coming up and he had a ring with a microscopic diamond in his pocket for when he'd given his news and he could officially ask her to marry him. He'd have asked the day after meeting her but he'd had nothing to offer.

He did now.

Like in a fairy tale, he and his princess would move and begin their lives together in a beautiful sunny kingdom far far away.

California.

She was working on a double major — Chinese studies and International Relations. She could do that just as well at Berkley as here. Better.

She'd come with him.

But first — he had to tell her his news.

Cal lifted his head then his torso up on his forearms. He kissed her forehead, pulled gently out of her. His dick complained, just like it always did because inside Anya was the best place to be. His dick hated pulling out.

But his dick could take a hike because there was serious stuff to talk about now.

"I have some news," he said softly, trying to keep the excitement out of his voice. Time for excitement later.

Anya pushed gently at his chest, their sign for him to get off her. When they were having sex, she said his weight on her was exciting. But he weighed almost double what she did and she always said that breathing was overrated when they were having sex, but became once again a priority post-sex.

Obediently, Cal rolled off her and she scooted up to sit against the plywood headboard, bunching pillows around her.

Oh man. She was just so beautiful sitting there, a naked princess with flat cheap pillows around her for a throne.

"So." She smiled at him. "What's the news? Is Kreizler going to let your name be on the paper?"

Cal frowned. Fuck, he'd forgotten about that. He'd done most of the work on a big paper on the elastic properties of graphene, staying up nights at the lab, laboriously recording tension and yield test results. Kreizler had made a half-assed promise that Cal's name would go on the paper but Cal had just seen the program for the World Conference of Materials Science to be held next March in Dublin and, nope. His name wasn't on the paper.

But that didn't make any difference now. He was going to leave Kreizler in the fucking dust. Leapfrog right over the bastard who treated him like hired help.

"Nah. He's not sharing. Didn't even have the nerve to tell me himself, I found out by checking the paper online. But, who the fuck cares?" He picked up her hand, soft and slender, and brought it to his mouth. "Because something better is on the horizon." He tried to control his breathing. "I got it. Anya, *I got it.*"

He was trying to keep the excitement down but his voice turned hoarse. He cleared his throat.

She took her other hand and smoothed away a lock of his too long hair. Damn, his hair grew out so fast and he didn't have the money to keep going to the barber. She smoothed the lock of hair behind his ear, still smiling gently at him. "Got what, darling?"

He was looking deep into her eyes but he closed his. He didn't want to watch her face when he told her the news because then ... well if she teared up then so would he and if he started crying the Man Police would rip his Y chromosome right out of him.

He swallowed heavily, held her hand tightly. "I got that post-doc fellowship at Stanford. Working with a top-tier research team headed by Habericht, who has a Nobel, and by Loren, who won a McArthur Genius Award three years ago. And that's not all. I got an offer from Benson Labs for a part time job that will become a full-time job after the fellowship. And the salary from Benson Labs will pay off my student loans in the first year."

He gave a sigh that came from deep in his chest. He was drowning in student debt.

This was like a dream come true. Cal smiled, opened his eyes — and froze.

Anya's lovely face was utterly blank. Not warm and welcoming, not happy for him, not anything. Just blank and ... cold?

What the fuck?

"Anya, honey, I —" But he didn't know what to say. Because all of a sudden, he wasn't touching her anymore and he hadn't moved. She had. She'd moved ... away from him.

And, oh fuck, she was out of bed, bending to pick up her clothes on the floor.

What had he said? Had he thought he'd told her about Stanford but instead something else had come out of his mouth? Had he had a stroke or been struck by one of those weird syndromes where only profanities came out of his mouth?

Fuck, no.

He remembered precisely what he'd said. *I got it.* Which was supposed to be her cue to cry out with joy and hug him and maybe he'd get another round of sex before asking her to marry him.

That was the way it was supposed to go. So what was happening right now? Something bad was happening, that was what. And he was powerless to stop it.

His muscles were paralyzed as he watched her pick up her dainty, lacy underwear from the floor. She always dressed simply. Bra, underpants, sweater, yoga pants, socks, boots and finally parka.

Cal was too dumbfounded to stop her, ask what she was doing. That was pointless anyway because it wasn't hard to figure out what she was doing. She was leaving. Instead of spending the night the way he'd hoped, she was going home.

He had just enough money left on his card to order pizzas in and the plan was to snuggle up with her and watch some pirated movie on his ancient laptop. It hadn't even occurred to him that that was not the way he was going to be spending his evening, the way he'd spent so many evenings. With her.

But she wasn't staying.

As she laced her boots he shook off the frozen spell he was under.

"What are you doing?" His voice croaked, cracked.

"Seems clear what I'm doing." Her own voice was cool, controlled.

"You're *leaving?*" The idea was still so strange he had to hear it from her mouth.

"That's right, ace. I'm leaving." She zipped up her parka, flipped up the hood and turned to face him. She was like ice. It was warm in his room but a chill emanated from her.

It was so unfair that she was still so beautiful, even somehow angry at him. The hood of the parka was lined with dark fake fur that looked like the real thing. It framed her face like that of a princess in a fairy tale, the kind where the princess wandered into the dark forest and made the big bad wolf fall in love with her.

Her beautiful face was closed to him, eyes like shards of ice.

What the fuck? *What was happening?*

He was getting screwed, is what was happening to him. And not in a good way. A spurt of anger flashed and he repressed it immediately. He'd never gotten angry at Anya, ever. And he wasn't going to start now. He didn't want to start now.

But ... what the fuck?

After staring at him coldly for a long moment, Anya turned on her heel and walked to the door. Opened it. Walked out.

Hell.

Cal stared at the door stupidly. His muscles felt slow, his brain felt mired in mud. He couldn't react. He could barely breathe.

What just happened? Was there a pod in the lavish wine cellars of her father's mansion, eating the real Anya after extruding a fake alien? No, that had been the real Anya he'd made love to. Her skin, the sounds she made, the way she clutched at him ... those were all real.

Loving Anya was the best thing that ever happened to him. She loved him right back, he was sure of it. They were young but neither of them were dummies. They'd lucked into true love at a young age but they both realized what they had. It was rare and precious and needed protecting.

He loved her and she loved him. Or, up until five minutes ago, she'd loved him. Then something ... changed.

Misery was setting in, a dark cloud of it rising like some dank fog from the nether regions of the earth. From caves and crevices where dark creatures dwelled. His head ached. His bones ached.

Too late, he realized he should be chasing her. Cal moved forward, but slowly and painfully, like he'd just taken a bad beating at the dojo. He was good in the dojo, it had been years since anyone had been able to hurt him. But this felt like he'd been beaten to within an inch of his life.

He'd opened his door and was walking out before he realized that he was buck naked. Much as he wanted to, he couldn't chase her like this. They'd arrest him. So he went back in, pulled up his jeans over his hips, jerked on his shirt without buttoning it and jammed his sockless feet into his ancient running shoes.

He limped down the stairs as if both legs had been broken. Something in him was broken. He threw open the front door of his apartment building and stared out in dismay. As usual, the light over the door and every other street light was out. He never let Anya walk alone after dark in his area. The fact that she had ... he couldn't go there. The idea that she'd rather court danger than stay with him was so painful he batted the thought away instantly.

It was snowing hard. Not pretty snowflakes gently settling on the cracked ground, but frozen rain flooding from the sky. He could see her boot prints but they disappeared two feet from the door. Right was a long slog to the subway, left was a bus stop. But she'd have to change three buses to get home. She usually took the subway. But never alone after dark, ever.

Her boot prints went to the right. She'd opted for the subway, which — damn it! — was not safe. Neither the streets to get there nor the station itself.

He took off running. He was a martial artist, not a track star. Cal was powerful, but not a runner. Still, he made good time, following her footsteps until he couldn't any more, the thick falling snow smudging them out.

But he knew the way to the subway and he ran as fast as he could.

She wasn't there. Cal frantically searched the filthy, graffiti-painted station. There were a couple of drug addicts, an ancient alcoholic preaching the end of the world and some tired workers.

Cal stared at the dirty station through eyes that stung, one hand braced against the wall as if he would fall down any second as he anxiously screened every passenger. Even when the train clanked in and came to a screeching stop, he studied everyone who boarded and stalked up and down the platform, peering into every car. On the crazy chance that she'd ... what? Run two miles to the previous station and gotten on there?

Well clearly she hadn't headed for the subway. Maybe she'd doubled back. Probably she'd called a cab. He hadn't even thought of that, because cabs never entered into his calculations. He could probably build a rocket to fly him to the moon before he could cab it everywhere.

Finally, he trudged up the stairs and out into the freezing cold. Fishing his cell out of his jeans, he thumbed her number. It was the first on his contacts list. The call went to voice mail.

The call went to voice mail all night. He must have called a hundred times but he never left a message, not trusting his voice.

The next day he called, then went to her apartment. Her father had bought her a pretty little studio apartment in a nice part of town. He stood at the front door ringing her bell for an hour until the super came out and chased him away.

The super's name was Mac, or that was what Cal called him. He was Polish and his name had enough consonants to sound like a sneeze. Cal and Mac were friends. Cal had helped him with building repairs a lot of times. But Mac wouldn't look him in the eye and pretended that his English had deserted him.

Cal called the mansion, though the idea of accidentally catching Mr. Voronov scared him. No danger of that, though. The housekeeper always answered, assuring him in icy tones that Miss Anya was not there, no she didn't know where Miss Anya was or when Miss Anya was coming back and by the way don't bother calling again.

He sent emails, pouring out his heart. She couldn't hear the tears in his voice in an email. But the emails remained unopened and never answered. Three days later, when he called her cell he got an announcement that the number was no longer in use.

He lost ten pounds that first week and missed all his classes. When he almost missed the deadline for accepting the job with Benson Labs, Cal knew that his future was on the line.

He could obsess over Anya and mourn her or he could get his act together and move forward.

He faxed his acceptance and bought the ticket to San Francisco with the last of the money in his bank account

Ten days after Anya walked out on him, on a bitterly cold, sleety day, Cal packed his few belongings and flew out West, toward his future.

Without Anya.

2

VENICE, ITALY, PALAZZO MALTESE

MARDI GRAS, TEN YEARS LATER

There was a woman dressed like that weird Star Wars queen, whatshername? Anakin Skywalker's wife. Amygdala? No that was a part of the brain. Amidala, that was it.

Though maybe Amygdala wasn't off the mark, since it was the part of the brain that governed lust and the lady at the masked ball was definitely making eyes at him. She had this enormous headdress, kabuki white makeup and a huge, red velvet cape that was open just enough to show her in a near transparent lace body stocking. She was holding a flute of champagne like everyone else and sipped from it without taking her eyes from his.

Then she blew him a kiss from overblown lips. Those lips were amazing, didn't even pretend to be natural, but promised a pretty decent blow job.

Nope, not interested.

Cal turned his back and looked out over the ballroom of Palazzo Maltese, where a thousand revelers were getting drunk and partying hard. A deluxe masked ball to celebrate the successful negotiation of the Mediterranean Accords, a multilateral agreement years in the making to establish peace and trade in the Middle East. After war had been tried, again and again, someone thought maybe peace might be worth a shot.

There was giddy jubilation in the air. It appeared that it had suddenly occurred to a lot of people that a brand new market of previously poor but now maybe future well-to-do people was opening up. Not only would there be peace, but there'd be money to be made. A lot of it.

Everyone who wasn't already drunk was doing his or her best to get there. Cal should be joining them. After years working in the Middle East with no alcohol at all, toiling at establishing desalination plants in desert environments, he deserved to get drunk.

Aside from other considerations, part of the Technical Dossier of the Accords was a contract with his company, Phoenix Enterprises, to provide safe drinking water for everyone, a dream in the desert that was thousands of years old.

And, not incidentally, he was about to become a billionaire. Officially. Not bad for a kid from the South Side. Mega-rich before he was forty. Doing good work, yet. Most billion-dollar fortunes were made trafficking in something or cheating people. Instead, his was going to be made saving lives.

Didn't get much better than that.

Now someone dressed as a super-sexy shepherdess was making eyes at him. This one dipped her finger in her champagne and ran it across breasts too good to be true. Those breasts were not made by God but by a skilled plastic surgeon.

Nuh uh. Not interested.

The fuck was wrong with him?

He'd worked practically his whole life to get to this point. He was richer than he'd ever dared dream, single after a brief marriage long ago to the she-devil from hell, in the most beautiful city in the world, at a party celebrating the breaking-out of peace, and he was turning down surefire sex? With champagne?

The hell?

Cal suppressed a sigh.

If only Anya — he stopped himself right there. *If only Anya* had been a constant thought in his life these past ten years. He'd married a banshee demon from hell because she'd looked a little like Anya. He'd turned down perfectly nice women because they didn't look like Anya.

Anya had left him *ten fucking years ago*. And she'd left him brutally, too.

He had to stop this, had to shake himself out of this melancholy mood. He was Cal Fucking Burns and he didn't do melancholy. He ran a hugely successful company with people hand-picked to be extremely competent and good to work with. His company was going to be instrumental in one of the greatest accomplishments in a hundred years, comparable to the signing of the Treaty of Versailles after World War I. An amazing achievement, one for the history books.

He was still young, physically strong, healthy and rich — and soon he was going to be much richer. So rich he wouldn't be able to spend all his money in a hundred lifetimes.

Shame on him. There was no room for sadness in a life like that.

He was highly sexed and he hadn't had sex in — he tried

to calculate it but couldn't remember. That had to stop, too. He was in a room full of beautiful women, and most of them looked pretty willing. There had to be someone here he wanted to fuck. Someone who *didn't* look like —

No. Not going there.

Huh. There was that redhead dressed in some outlandish rendering of what some might consider Marie Antoinette if Marie Antoinette had a gown cut down to the tops of her nipples.

Well, nothing ventured nothing gained. Cal started off toward the redhead, wondering if she spoke English. Maybe she didn't. Maybe that would make it better. Just find a place to fuck without talking. Maybe not even take their masks off.

Something grabbed at his sleeve and, annoyed, Cal looked down. A long, slim, pale hand. He followed that hand up to the face and grew even more annoyed.

"Enjoying yourself?" a light, affected voice asked.

Shit, just perfect. To add to his mild depression, he had been caught by the biggest asshole-bore in the world. Tall, slender, blonde hair combed straight back, dressed as a 17th-century swordsman. A musketeer. Which was rich considering he was a total wimp. Calvin had saved his ass in Cairo and Damascus.

Ashley Morris, in the flesh, come to pester Cal. What was he doing here anyway? Ash worked for the CIA, which just showed how low their standards had fallen. Ash and the CIA had done their best to assist the negotiation of the Accords by fucking things up more than once.

"How are you doing? I heard Phoenix cleaned up, landed a huge contract. How does it feel to be mega-rich?" Ash asked.

So — they were playing catch-up?

"Pretty good," Cal said mildly. He was technically already a billionaire now if you counted his stock in Phoenix and he would be a bi-billionaire very soon. Ash wouldn't care. He was a trustafarian from old money and had joined the CIA because he thought it made him look dashing. It didn't. He just looked like a moron, playing out of his weight class. He still looked like a kid. "And you? What are you doing here?"

"Well." Ash drew himself up, putting a hand on the hilt of his sword. He gave a smug smile. "I played a small part in the accords," he said, shrugging his shoulders, humblebragging. His tone suggested that the multilateral negotiations, a major historical breakthrough in diplomacy, wouldn't have happened without him.

"Good for you." Cal snagged another glass of champagne from a passing waiter in livery, drank it in three long gulps. He needed fortification if he had to talk to Ash.

"Yes." Ash pursed his lips. "We ... facilitated backdoor talks. Enormous geopolitical considerations. It wasn't all as straightforward and simple as landing an engineering contract."

Cal placed the empty flute on another passing waiter's tray and turned his head to look at Ash who was still babbling.

What Cal and his company had done was the private sector equivalent to the moonshot on an accelerated schedule. He and his team had worked tirelessly under conditions of extreme privation, solving one thorny, impossible technical problem after another. They'd built a demo desalination plant in Yemen on time and under budget before the ceasefire, under mortar attack and with constant attempts at sabotage. Though Cal had arranged tight security, he'd lost two engineers to an IED.

But every engineer in the company insisted on seeing the project through to the end, and they'd landed the big contract to provide safe and clean drinking water throughout the Middle East.

They'd created a fucking miracle that was going to save hundreds of thousands of lives, maybe millions of lives, and it hadn't been straightforward and it hadn't been simple. Cal and his team had worked like dogs, in 120° heat, eating goat meat when they were lucky, dodging bullets when they weren't.

And Ash probably sat the whole thing out in some air-conditioned office playing with his tiny dick.

Something in Cal's face made Ash flinch. "Yeah. So." He huffed out a breath, looked around casually over Cal's shoulder. Great. Ash was one of those cocktail party people who looked over your shoulder for someone more interesting to talk to while talking to you.

Cal could solve that problem for him, easy.

"Well." He plastered a smile on his face. "Great catching up with you, Ash. I think I'll —"

His arm was caught in a weak grip. Cal looked at the hand and at Ash's face. Ash dropped his hand but stepped closer, right into what Cal considered his personal space. He didn't like it when the wrong people stepped into his personal space.

Ash definitely qualified.

It took a lot of self control not to deck the fuckhead. The fact that it would be all too easy to flatten him kept him still but, man, was he tempted.

"Anya." Ash had been talking and Cal hadn't been paying any attention to him, but that word made him stiffen. Had he heard right?

"What? What did you say?"

Ash sighed. "I said have you seen Anya Voronova anywhere?"

Cal's neurons stopped firing. It was like hearing someone talking from far away. "What?"

"Anya. Voronova." Ash's voice was exasperated. "Anya. Come on, I know you know her. Didn't you guys date, like, a billion years ago?"

Cal's lips felt stiff, wooden. He formed words with difficulty. "Anya is *here*?"

Ash's eyes were moving restlessly over the crowd. But now they honed in on his face. "Why shouldn't she be? She's deputy director of Peace and Jobs. Of course she's here."

Peace and Jobs was one of a number of NGOs that had worked hard to secure the Accords, working under the umbrella Diplomatic Dossier. Peace and Jobs worked in the background, an organization with a sterling reputation. Cal had never had dealings with Peace and Jobs but he'd certainly heard of them.

Anya was deputy director?

"I only met her once back in the day," Ash said. "Wouldn't recognize her now. And all I have is this." He held out his cell that showed an ID. Cal's heart gave a painful kick in his chest. Oh fuck. *There she was.*

Ten years older and about a million times more beautiful even though it was a work ID, face full on, harsh lighting, no makeup, hair drawn back from her face. Anya's face was no longer girlish. It was a woman's face — intelligent and determined.

Cal stared at the photo, soaking in every pixel. In all these years he deliberately hadn't looked for her, hadn't tried to keep up, hadn't Googled her, ever. Once he started, he'd never stop. His heart was already broken, no point in smashing it to bits.

In his head, he'd convinced himself she'd left because he'd never have been able to give her the lifestyle she'd been born to, even though that was insane. Anya had never given any sign of caring that he had no money. But how else to understand what had happened in his miserable hovel on a snowy afternoon? The love of his life just walking out on him.

In his head, he'd convinced himself that she was bound to marry some fourth generation rich guy and lead a pampered life. But the face he was looking at wasn't pampered, wasn't botoxed or surgically enhanced. It had lines and the hint of shadows under her eyes, as if she'd been working too hard.

Well, yeah. If she was Deputy Director of Peace and Jobs she'd been working nonstop for years.

Ash bobbed his head to indicate the crowd. There wasn't a woman there who didn't have a mask and wasn't wearing a costume, most very elaborate. Some were completely hidden behind the classic Venetian porcelain masks. Ash tapped his cell screen. "My facial recognition app won't work here. Not enough identifying data points."

Ash's face tightened and he finally looked adult. A nasty adult, thoroughly grown up.

Cal nearly did a double take. "Why are you looking for Anya? Is anything wrong?"

Ash shrugged. "I came into some information today that she absolutely needs to know. Don't know her cell number, the offices of Peace and Jobs aren't picking up, she's not answering email. But I know she's here. She has to be. Larry Silver, her boss, is apparently out of town, won't get here until the signing ceremony tomorrow, and she has to be here, to represent Peace and Jobs." His eyes slid to Cal's. "It's really important. Think you can find her for me?"

Could he find Anya in a crowd of strangers? Hell yeah. He could recognize Anya anywhere, even at a hundred paces, even after a hundred years, even dressed in a burqa. Though he'd tried to uproot her, cast her out, she was buried deep in his heart and he was sure there would be an instant recognition if he ever saw her again. Cal hated it, but his heart was beating triple time at the thought of seeing Anya again.

Even more, he hated to admit to himself that any time he'd been Stateside in the past five years, he'd unconsciously searched every crowd for a cap of shiny gold hair and piercing blue eyes. He hated crowds and that was one of the main reasons.

Because Anya was never there.

Though he never knew what he'd do if by some miracle she actually was in that crowd. It had taken him years before he could think of her without a stab to the heart. And further years before a day or sometimes even two would go by without her popping up in his head.

As a matter of fact, he'd welcomed these past five years of brutal, unremitting, dangerous work in Yemen, then a desolate part of Morocco, then Iraq and Syria. Getting up before sunrise and collapsing onto a cot long after the sun went down, falling unconscious rather than falling asleep. The work — physically and mentally strenuous — had scrubbed her at least partially from his heart.

He wasn't over her and he imagined that maybe he'd never be over her. He could see himself in some hospital in extreme old age, dying, and wondering whether she was in the same hospital.

Sometimes Cal wondered whether his DNA had been changed by falling so deeply in love at such a young age. Whether his heart became a lock and only Anya had the key.

And she'd thrown it away.

He'd tried his best to think of her as little as possible, because at first a deep black pall and then years later a gray pall descended on him whenever he pictured her. He had wonderful memories of their time together. They'd done everything a young couple in love could do when there was no money. Well, Anya had had money, true, but Cal wouldn't let her pay for anything. So it was long walks in the park and picnics on the Common and a lot of sex at his place. But what always popped up was the memory of that terrible day when she left. When she shattered his heart and he hadn't understood why.

He still didn't understand why.

But now — well now it looked like for the first time since that day, he was in the *same building* as Anya. Breathing the same air she was. Cal walked forward, aware that he'd been scanning the crowd since the moment Ash mentioned her name. Head on a swivel, Cal made his way through the crowd.

All his senses were assaulted. There were three huge chandeliers casting a light almost as bright as the sun. Thousands of people were talking excitedly, vying with the small chamber orchestra set up on a podium at the far end of the ballroom. The perfume and sweat of a thousand people mixed with the scents of food on platters being circulated together with champagne. All the costumes were brightly colored, as were many of the masks.

The entire reception was a riot of sound and color and smells and looking for one person in this crowd seemed like an impossibility. But Anya was somewhere here and he wasn't leaving before seeing her, talking to her.

If this had been anything but a party and he was looking for an object in a big space full of objects, he'd have divided the room into a grid and searched it systematically. But the place was crowded and people moved constantly in a speeded-up Brownian motion. Everyone seemed to be on the make, looking for another drink, another bite to eat, another person other than the one they were talking to.

Everyone was restless, agitated, hyped up. It was an historic occasion and if you weren't drunk on the champagne you were drunk on the moment.

There was no way to search systematically so he just bulled his way from one end to the other, head on a swivel, watching carefully to his left and right. The costumes were amazing, mostly a reproduction of what he understood to be Venice's heyday, the 17th century. So there were a lot of shepherdesses and elaborate ballroom gowns and men in livery. But there was a lot of cosplay, too. He saw several Wonder Women, two Batmen and a couple of T'Challas, the Black Panther.

And that was just by the drinks station.

God, how would she be dressed? What would Anya choose as a costume? When they'd been together, Cal could have confidently come up with a couple of ideas she might have, but now? It was ten years later. People changed a lot in ten years.

He only hoped she wasn't wearing one of those porcelain

masks that completely covered the face except for the eyes. Her eyes were immediately recognizable but if she was wearing the porcelain mask and contact lenses ...

Never mind. He'd recognize her by her stance, by her perfume, by the aura around her.

He was dressed in the least costume-y thing he could come up with — as the Phantom of the Opera. He was wearing one of his designer tuxes and one of his engineers had 3-D laser printed the Phantom half mask that fit his face perfectly.

Nobody gave him a second look as he scoured the ground floor of the immense Palazzo. He made his way across the enormous space once then back, like wading through a huge lake of costumed humans.

She wasn't here. But there were three other floors, a ballroom, and a bridge thirty feet in the air over a side canal led to another palazzo.

It seemed like everyone who'd ever been involved in the multiparty, multistate Accords, thousands of people over the years, was here, ready to party.

Well, if Anya was here, Cal was going to find her. He'd stayed out of her orbit — never dreaming over the past years that they had been working on the same project, though far apart — but if she was here already, he couldn't be accused of stalking her.

Because fuck, he'd wanted to. He'd moved cross-country only because he'd had to, and almost every single fucking day for years, particularly after he started earning serious money, he'd wanted to board a plane and seek her out. Which would have been a disaster. He'd avoided Boston, he'd avoided the whole fucking east coast, as a result. He'd gone from Stanford, to Benford Labs, to founding his own company in California, to the Middle East, without ever setting foot in New England because if he had, the temptation to seek her out would have been too strong.

And he'd stayed off the internet. He was good with computers and he'd written a little program that created static whenever he typed Anya Voronova in any search engine. Otherwise he'd have followed her every move and driven himself crazy.

But hell. She was here, right now. And he had a reason to seek her out, a legitimate one, even if the reason was that asshole Ash.

He started up the curving monumental staircase, with marble steps and polished teak balustrade, halting halfway up to look down on the revelers. From this vantage point he could see every corner of the huge hall. He was used to measuring, surveying, so he pulled up a mental grid of the room and quartered it, fast.

No Anya.

On up.

The monumental staircase gave onto huge glass doors. He pushed through them into a large frescoed room. He could see another set of doors across the room. There were slightly fewer people on the second floor, though it was still crowded. He'd refined his search parameters and could literally not see the people outside them. Men — eliminated from his scan. Too short and too tall women — the same. There were still a lot of potential Anyas but fewer.

Cal was tunnel-visioning now, barely seeing waiters holding out silver trays of food and champagne, noticing the string quartet at the end of the long hallway only glancingly.

He powered his way across the room and pushed open the doors into what looked like a fantasy land. It was a large hallway with an arcade, ringed by torches, elaborate frescoes covering every inch. Cherubs and shepherds and shepherdesses and goddesses. Huge, antique, enameled vases lined the marble-tiled floor, planted with tall palms interspersed with flowering shrubs, deeply scented. The arcade gave out onto an inner courtyard where another string quartet was playing and the sounds of Vivaldi drifted up, as in a dream.

There were fewer people in this room and Cal could see right down to the end. Nothing. Except …

There was a hidden alcove to the right. Someone had been standing in the alcove and now emerged into the hallway. A woman, dressed as a 1920s flapper. A dress with jet beads, just above her knees. Black hair in a short bob, a velvet hat with a net veil covering her face. Anya didn't have black hair, her hair was honey blonde, but …

There was something about the way this woman moved.

There was something in the air in this corridor. It was charged, electric. There was a scent in the air, a mix of lavender and citrus, fresh and sultry at the same time. A scent that intoxicated.

Cal found himself moving faster and faster down the hallway. He'd worked in very dangerous places over the course of the years and he'd learned to move swiftly and very silently. It was second nature by now.

He was more than halfway down when the woman turned and he saw the sky blue eyes that glowed beneath the black lace veil.

His heart thundered and his breath grew short.

Anya.

3

Anya Voronova was sorry she'd come to the crowded masked ball. If her boss at Peace and Jobs hadn't been detained in Cairo, she'd have cried off. Simply refused to go. Larry knew her well and knew what he was asking of her. But he'd had to stay a day over in Cairo and someone had to represent Peace and Jobs at the celebratory ball. Looked like that someone was her.

She knew that it was a privilege. The Palazzo was an exquisite work of art, the food was amazing, the music was fabulous. Even the people looked intriguing — though she knew a great number of them and many were greedy, grasping bastards, when they weren't violent monsters.

But ... peace had broken out. A few good men and women in a few good governments had worked really hard to create a system where it was worth everyone's while to make peace rather than war.

And a lot of people were going to make a lot of money, most of them reluctantly accepting wealth in lieu of thousand-year hatreds, but doing it nonetheless. Maybe their great great grandchildren would forget about the thousand-year-old hatreds.

Good old greed, she thought, as she had thought many times before. It was better than hate.

She and the small staff at Peace and Jobs, together with about fifty other NGOs, had worked tirelessly for the greatest diplomatic achievement in living memory.

She should have enjoyed dressing up in something other than jeans and sweatshirt and ball cap, her uniform in the field. Enjoyed putting on a costume, mingling with people who didn't have to be coaxed and persuaded to rebuild schools and hospitals in the rubble of their cities. Enticed into not hating their neighbors.

She sighed and pinched the bridge of her nose through the veil. Dressing like a 1920s flapper had been her little sign of rebellion since most everyone was dressed in 17th-century costume, maybe in a subconscious attempt to forget what the modern world was like.

Wow.

Was she in a sour mood. Maybe she was tired, that was it. What other reason could she have for not enjoying a brilliant masked ball celebrating something she and her colleagues had been working toward for years? Something that would have been considered impossible just a few years ago.

Or maybe it was because she was alone here, though that was entirely her fault. Or rather — fault wasn't maybe the right term. It was just that of the many invitations she'd had, none had appealed. Even her boss had made it clear that he'd like for there to be something more than friendship between them.

But luckily he was also the sort of guy to step back as soon as she made her lack of interest clear.

The others — not so much.

What was *wrong* with her? She could have her pick of men and she never picked one. Or rarely did. The last date she'd been on was — she had to actually focus to remember — in Amman. The US Embassy trade attaché. Nice, not unhandsome, very interested and very boring. No spark there at all.

She hadn't been really interested in anyone since ... her mind skittered away from that name, as it always did. But she was too tired to force herself not to think of *him*.

Cal.

Calvin Burns. Maybe the love of her life. Not the one who got away but the one she'd let get away. The man she'd tossed away years ago.

There'd really been no one since and how pathetic was that? There'd been lovers of course. A couple where she thought they could fill the Cal-shaped hole in her heart, but they never could. At one point, crying on the couch after she'd sent away a perfectly nice but not-Cal man, she'd wondered whether she was cursed. Whether that long-ago gesture, forced on her, spelled her doom. That she was destined to spend her years on this earth in solitude.

But she was Russian in blood only. That was the kind of thinking of her ancestors — that our lives are fated to follow a pre-ordained destiny. That our blood determined whether we'd have happy or tragic lives.

No, she was thoroughly American, convinced that people shaped their own lives.

So why was she so freaking unhappy?

Why did she look for him in every crowd? Maybe that

was why she was up here all alone, so she wouldn't find herself in the ballroom scanning for a tall man with sandy hair and light brown eyes like an eagle's, as she had so many times before. Even though it was absurd to think of him being here, in Venice, at this celebration of the Accords.

He was almost certainly back in California, with his wife. Nine years ago, the instant she'd been free to do so, she'd flown to Palo Alto, to see if he could forgive her. It had been crazy, she'd known it was crazy, but had been helpless to stop herself.

She'd actually seen him in her first half hour in town, holding hands with a beautiful blonde sporting a huge diamond ring. She'd turned around and taken the first flight back to Boston from SFO. The internet told her everything she needed to know. Checking up on him, she read the announcement of his marriage.

She took a vow then to never check up on him ever again, and kept it.

She applied for a job with the new NGO Peace and Jobs that promised hard work and travel. Perfect.

So why was she thinking so hard about Cal right now? Why ...

Her skin prickled. Sweat broke out on her back, though the hallway was cool. Her heart started pounding as some kind of band tightened around her chest.

What the hell?

Was this a heart attack? A stroke? She felt dizzy, as if she might stumble and fall at any minute.

It was like the molecules of the air were charged with electric static. The hairs on her forearms rose, she felt pressure on the nape of her neck.

Maybe it was danger. These past years had been spent in

some very dangerous places and she prided herself on her street smarts. Maybe there was a threat to her and her body was letting her know.

Anya turned around slowly, sorry that she hadn't thought to bring her pepper spray with her. The only thing in her jet-bead-embroidered clutch was lipstick, her hotel card key, two €50 notes and her cell.

So she turned, ready to shuck her shoes and run. She was fast and the building was crowded. She could outrun danger.

But when she turned, she realized she couldn't outrun this danger.

Before her was a tall, well-built man, very tan, short sandy hair, light brown eyes fierce and cold.

He was in costume, sort of. A well-cut black tuxedo, stiff white pleated shirt, cummerbund, black tie. Half his face was covered with a white Phantom of the Opera mask, but she'd recognize him anywhere.

Cal. Calvin Burns, after all these years. All grown up.

He'd been a good-looking young man, but now he was devastating. Leaner, but bulked up in the shoulders that strained against the tux. Formal wear suited him, even as the elegant evening wear contrasted with his very tan, weather-beaten face. The last time she'd seen him his dark blonde hair had fallen to his shoulders. He'd worn his hair long mainly because he couldn't afford to go to a barber often. Now his hair was buzzed short, so short she could see his scalp.

"Cal?" she whispered.

He nodded, face grim.

It seemed so strange, him here. She reached out a hand then let it drop. "Is it really you?"

He nodded again.

"What are you doing here?"

"What?" His mouth tightened. "You don't think I'm good enough to be here?"

"*What?*" She was shocked. When she tried to pull in air it wasn't there. "No, not at all! How can you say that?"

It was as if he hadn't heard her. He stepped forward, close enough that she had to look up to meet his eyes. Had he grown in the past ten years?

"I have as much right to be here as you do," he said, his tone belligerent.

"Of course. I — ah ..."

Her brain just switched off. He was looking at her so intently, light brown eyes fierce, locked onto hers. He was so different from the young man — a boy, really — she remembered so well. Anya had dreamed of him so many times and in her dreams he was the boy she'd left all those years ago.

But this was a different person, and he was all man. Lean, hardened, cold.

The old Cal, *her* Cal, had been basically a puppy. A big, enthusiastic puppy, eager to please, always happy. She couldn't ever remember him frowning.

This Cal looked like he'd never smiled in his life.

She'd thought of him, dreamed of him, yearned for him over the years. Though the days were for working on the big Peace and Jobs project, The Accords, her nights were for dreaming. She'd dreamt of seeing Cal again, a suddenly unmarried and unencumbered Cal, and of them getting together again. She'd dreamed it so often that in her fantasies, the preliminaries disappeared, there was no run-up. There was just her and Cal, together again, the past wiped out.

She'd pleasured herself to the thought of being in Cal's arms again countless times.

It was easy to take a step forward, instinctively, arms coming up for an embrace.

He didn't step back but he did stiffen and his entire body turned into a no-touching zone.

Okay okay. *Got it.* She'd given up the right to touch him ten years ago. Her fingers curled into the palms of her hands.

They stood watching each other. Anya felt frozen. She couldn't breathe, she couldn't move, had no idea what to do.

Oh God he looked so *good.* She gulped up all the details as quickly as she could, trying not to stare.

He had some Slavic blood in him — Cal always said he was a mutt while she was a purebred — and in his younger days his face had been wide, like a pale, friendly moon.

Not now. Now his brown face was drawn, with high, chiseled cheekbones, hollow cheeks, lean and grim. His body, too, was completely different. He'd been blocky from all the martial arts he did, but he wasn't blocky now. He had massive shoulders and chest which narrowed down to a lean waist and long, strong legs.

The tux fit him like a dream.

Anya tried really hard not to check him out head to toe in an obvious way, but her eyes did stop on his left hand.

No ring.

He was married. Why wasn't he wearing a ring?

She was staring. *Say something!* She told herself.

"I —"

"What —"

They both spoke at once. People smiled when that happened, but Cal didn't smile. He moved his big, tanned hand in an *after you* gesture.

Anya had no idea what she wanted to say. Or rather, there were so many things jostling in her head, buzzing like angry bees. What to say first?

How are you? Where have you been? Why are you here and no, I don't think you don't belong here, why should I? But — did you work on the Accords? Are you part of this? Why haven't I seen you? Where do you live now?

Where's your wife?

No, she couldn't ask that.

She opened her mouth to say something bland but a laughing group of cosplayers turned the corner and filled the hallway with shrieks and comments in four languages. As they passed by, the air was thick with scents — perfumes and brandy. It was traditional in Venice during Mardi Gras to dress in 17th-century costume, when Venice was la Serenissima — one of the world's major superpowers. But they hadn't gotten the memo and there was a Harley Quinn, a Wonder Woman, a Princess Leia, a Batman and two Jokers.

They were loud and raucous and made noise all the way down the hallway toward the monumental staircase.

"Is there somewhere we can talk?" Cal asked, scowling.

"Yes." She'd worked for months in Palazzo Maltese and knew every single room in the huge building.

In the old days, she'd have grabbed Cal's hand but that was now off limits. So she merely nodded at him, turned around and walked to the end of the hallway. He was following her. She knew this because of the electrical charge in the air, not because she heard him. He was completely silent as he walked, whereas her twenties shoes with the silk bow ties were loud in the sudden silence. The raucous party had reached the other end of the hallway and walked through the big doors into the larger room. The sounds of the party flowed through when the doors opened, then dulled again as they closed.

Anya turned right and tested the brass handle of the second door to the left. Maybe they had sealed off some of the rooms that weren't suited to the revelry? But no, the door opened easily and she stood aside as Cal entered the room, looking around.

It was a lovely room, as all the rooms in Palazzo Maltese were. Intimate, decorated with priceless antiques, frescoed. There was an enormous 18th-century table in the center with delicate, silk-upholstered armchairs around it, which made it a meeting room. Anya had had numerous meetings here. Someone had held a meeting earlier in the evening because a sideboard held an ice bucket full of melting ice and three bottles of champagne and there were platters of canapés on end tables.

Cal took in the room at a glance and headed for the sideboard, yanking off his half mask on the way. "Champagne?" he asked, his hand hovering over the bucket.

Alcohol? After seeing the love of her life after a ten-year absence? God yes!

"Yes, thank you." She kept her voice low because there was something about Cal that was like an explosive device just waiting to detonate. She didn't want to be what set him off but she feared she would be.

There was a quiet pop as he uncorked the champagne. He poured her a flute and held it out by the stem. She took it from him without touching his fingers. He poured himself a glass, gulped it down fast, then poured another one.

And that's when she noticed his hands. They were trembling. You could barely see it, but the liquid in the flute made little waves.

Cal Burns' hands were trembling.

Impossible. The Cal Burns she knew was the steadiest human being she'd ever met, including her father who'd had nerves of steel. Maybe it was basically growing up in a dojo, maybe it was having to make his own way in the world completely on his own, but whatever the reason, Cal had turned himself into a machine with a big heart. He wasn't intimidated by anything, he wasn't afraid of anything. He relished challenge.

Yet his hands were trembling slightly.

She did this to him. His hands were trembling because of her.

It emboldened her. She stepped forward. One step, to see how he reacted.

He flinched. It was so subtle it could hardly be seen, but she saw. She saw because she knew him so very well. Ten years separated them, a gulf of time, but people didn't change all that much. Cal hadn't flinched, ever, when he was a poor student carrying two jobs, a full student load, and a ton of student debt, always one step away from absolute penury.

This Cal looked prosperous. That was an Armani tuxedo he was wearing, unless she missed her guess. And if he was here, he was one of the world's elite. The Accords were the biggest international event in the past hundred years. To be here was to have status.

Cal had never flinched when he'd been poor and powerless.

So if Cal flinched now ...

She took another step forward and he gulped his second glass of champagne as if it were water.

She still meant something to him. He still had feelings

for her. Those feelings might be anger or even hatred, but they were there.

And oh God, she had feelings for him. She'd never stopped, not for a second.

Another step forward and he drew himself up to his full height. She had to tilt her head back to look him in the eyes. Those bright, fierce, almost yellow eyes she'd loved to gaze into.

A sudden flashback. They were in his studio apartment, making love. He was always so ashamed of his place. It was dingy, with thin walls, chilly in the winter, steaming in the summer. But he kept it spotlessly clean and she hadn't cared at all about the miserable surroundings, as long as she was with him.

The room and the whole world disappeared anyway when they were having sex.

She remembered, as clearly as if it had been yesterday, when he entered her. He was big, and it was always a tight fit right at the start and she had to consciously relax to accommodate him. And he always stopped, just inside her, to give her time. But that time they'd had extensive foreplay and he was really aroused and so was she and he slid inside her to the hilt right away.

He was on top. They experimented, but they both liked it when he was on top. His face was an inch from hers, their noses touched. When he realized that he'd slid right in, his eyes had widened. When they were making love there seemed to be a light inside his head and his eyes just glowed like a tiger's in the night.

That time she'd locked eyes with his and it had been like nothing she'd ever experienced before. Magnetic and almost scary. She'd started shaking and had started coming as soon as he moved, an explosive orgasm that left her gasping and trembling. And that whole time, those tiger eyes had never left hers.

She remembered it. And how. Her body remembered that time, too. Her treacherous, treacherous body. It was like a fire had started inside her, heat exploding outward, burning up all the oxygen in her lungs. The sound of her gasping for breath was loud in the room. Her skin prickled. She could feel the material of her costume rasping against super-sensitized skin, though the costume was the smoothest silk possible. It felt like her bra and panties suddenly shrank several sizes. Her breasts felt heavy, the nipples brushing against the lace bra, so tender it almost hurt.

Oh God, could he tell just by looking at her how turned on she was? She'd almost forgotten this feeling. The few lovers she'd had since Cal had never excited her like this, not even close. She hadn't felt like this since — since Cal.

She took another gasp of air, as if she were drowning. It couldn't be helped, the air in the room didn't seem to be enough.

Her knees trembled.

Anya had spent the past nine years in rooms with men who disliked her, personally and because of her gender, men who hated everything she stood for, who despised her for being a woman, a Westerner, in a position of power.

She'd long ago learned to control every aspect of her outward appearance, to remain cool and calm in negotiations between parties that had hated each other for a thousand years, bitter enmity poisoning the air. Yet here she was, spiraling out of control, her body betraying her because of an old lover.

She couldn't do this. She shouldn't do this. Their break was her fault, but the Anya of ten years ago no longer existed. And the Cal Burns of ten years ago definitely no longer existed.

He'd never looked at her with anything less than warm love in his gaze. Now his eyes were cold and flat, unreadable.

They were staring at each other, unblinking. She had to break this spell.

"So —" Anya gestured with her glass, misjudging. A little champagne sloshed over the top. Cal didn't even seem to notice. His eyes were locked on hers. "What *are* you doing here?"

Cal shook his head sharply, like someone waking out of a trance. "Phoenix." His voice was cold, deep, clipped. "Phoenix Enterprises."

"Phoenix? I, ah, I don't —" and then she did understand. The Accords consisted of a million moving parts. One of those parts, which she'd never had dealings with because they were part of the Technical Dossier, was a big corporation called Phoenix Enterprises, providing safe desalinated water to the Middle East. "So — you work for Phoenix Enterprises?"

"No." He stopped, jaws working.

"No?" He looked *angry*. So angry. What had she said? Something about Phoenix Enterprises had set him off. Maybe she should change the subject. Her mouth opened and she had to trust that something would fill the silence. But then he spoke.

"Phoenix Enterprises. It's mine."

Her eyes widened. Phoenix Enterprises was *Cal's*? Oh God. It was one of the great companies of the world — right up there with Microsoft and Apple and Google. Maybe more important because it was saving lives. Drought was no longer a scourge. For the first time in history, water was no longer a fighting issue, something people died for.

A great rush of emotion went through her, a flood of pure pride. Cal had started life with nothing, but he'd always had outsized smarts and courage and ambition. But this — this was amazing. Gone was the memory of their breakup and of the last ten long and lonely years. Something in her heart brightened. The boy she'd loved so much had turned into a remarkable man. Cal had worked a miracle.

She reached out to him instinctively, touching his forearm. "Oh my gosh, Cal! How amazing!"

It had come straight from the heart, but his heart was unmoved. He jerked back as if she had Ebola that could be transmitted by touch. As if her touch could taint him, burn him.

Well, that pain had to be just tucked away, didn't it? She deserved that. It hurt, but then a lot of things in life hurt.

Her hand dropped. She made it look natural, not as if it broke her heart, just a little, not to be able to touch him. Diplomatic training took over and instead of snatching her hand back, she waved it at the couch. "Should we sit down?"

His jaw muscles clenched again. Clearly he didn't want to sit down, not with her at any rate. He looked like he didn't want to be in the same room with her, in the same building, in the same city.

Anya's heart broke just a little bit more. Tears burned at the backs of her eyes but she'd be damned if she'd let any of that show.

He didn't want to sit with her, but she wanted to sit with him. The hell with it. Ten years had gone by and maybe this would be the last time in this lifetime that she'd be next to him again. No matter the blow to her pride, she needed this.

A part of her realized that she was storing up memories that she'd take out again and again in the future. The smell of him, the heat his big body generated, that handsome, lean face, those huge shoulders, all encased in a gorgeous black tuxedo.

She sat, the jet beads rustling, tinkling. When she chose this dress, sitting hadn't been part of the plan. It was necessary for her to take part in the huge Mardi Gras party celebrating the Accords but the plan had been to stand, mingle, drink some champagne and then, when everyone was too soused to notice, leave quietly.

The last thing she expected was to come across Cal Burns.

He sat stiffly, muscles tense, a scowl between his eyebrows. He was sitting on the edge of the pretty brocaded couch, almost quivering with eagerness to get away.

Oh God. If only she could stop time! Just stop it, like in the movies. Press pause. He would freeze, and then she could look at him to her heart's content. And oh, she just wanted to gobble up every detail. To compare the man in front of her with the boy she'd carried in her heart all these years.

Cal used to wear his hair long. He'd just let it grow. It made him look a little like a Viking, scruffy and rough. Now he had what must have been a $300 haircut, so precise it could have been done by laser. She hadn't appreciated how well-shaped his head was when he had hair down to his shoulders, but this cut showed off the clean lines of his head and face.

As a student, Cal had bothered to shave only a couple of

times a week and there was always a sandy scruff covering his jaw. Now his face gleamed from a very close shave.

His face had narrowed, hollowed under sharp cheekbones. Lines fanned out from his eyes in his sun-tanned face.

And his body. Oh man. He'd been a buff young man — he'd practically grown up in a dojo and he'd been strong and muscled. This man looked lethal — sharper, cut and infinitely dangerous.

Age had only added to his appeal, not taken anything away. Plus he had this hard and commanding air, as if he'd been slaying dragons all this time. Well, if he had founded Phoenix and made it into what it was today, he really had been slaying dragons.

Oh how she *wished* she'd been at his side, helping him create Phoenix and watching it grow. They'd have done it together. She didn't know anything about engineering or desalination but she was good at public relations. They'd have made the most amazing team ...

But that was crazy thinking. She'd left him and he'd done all of it on his own, without her. Hating her every step of the way, it seemed.

It was unbearable to have him hating her, not knowing the truth. What had seemed so compelling at the time, her iron-clad duty, her desire to safeguard his future, now seemed like pale morning mist, easily dissipated. Her heart had broken that day and he hadn't known it.

Suddenly, it was imperative that he know the truth. She couldn't keep silent one minute longer. When her father had died and the sale had been complete and the two thousand jobs secured, she'd actually trekked out to Stanford to tell him. To throw herself on his mercy, beg forgiveness. Do whatever it took to get back together again. Pay for what she'd done for the rest of her life, if necessary. Gladly. Just as long as they could be together.

Being without him had been torture. She'd survived simply because she'd been working so hard to take care of her father and the company. But not a minute went by when she didn't miss him.

And when she'd finally been free to go out to Palo Alto, she'd seen him, arm around a beautiful woman.

Laughing. And with a ring on his finger and a ring on hers.

Back home, she'd applied to a new NGO, Peace and Jobs. The post demanded long hours which sounded fantastic. She wanted to drown herself in work. And the job involved a lot of travel, which was fine. She'd welcomed that.

And she only just now realized that all that travel had been to keep her far away from Cal Burns. The irony was he'd been working on the same project all this time.

There were things that had to be said. She had to explain to him what she'd done and why. So she surprised herself when she said, "Are you with your wife here?"

Only long training kept her from clapping her hand over her mouth.

The scowl deepened. "What?" He'd been staring stonily at the opposite wall but he suddenly turned his face to hers, his eyes burning. "My what?"

"Wife." Anya wanted to be self-confident and matter-of-fact but the word came out strangled. "Your wife," she clarified.

"I don't have a wife." He said the words clearly and coldly.

"But — but I thought —" Anya cleared her throat. She couldn't possibly say, *Yes, you do, I saw her.*

If anything Cal's voice turned even colder. "I was briefly married nine years ago. The marriage didn't last. Not that it's any of your business."

Anya waited. Waited for him to ask the obvious question. *And you? Are you married?*

But he wasn't asking. He was doing an excellent imitation of a wooden statue. An enormously handsome wooden statue.

There was a long and awkward silence. Cal downed another flute of champagne, put the flute carefully on a small, elaborately-inlaid 18th-century side table and clapped his knees. "Well."

His entire body language screamed *get me out of here.* He stood up and Anya panicked. *No, no, no. He couldn't go now!* Not yet. There was too much she had to know. Too much he had to know. She reached out and grasped his hand. "No, please don't go."

He looked down at his hand, with her hand clasping it, then back up to her face. Under her palm, Anya could feel the very fine tremor, barely there. More a vibration than anything else. He wasn't quite as unaffected as he was pretending to be.

His look was cold, steely. With a huge pang, Anya remembered a time when she was welcome to touch Cal anywhere, in any way, at any time. Those days were gone.

Maybe.

"I know you want to get away, but I need you to listen to me."

"You *need* me to listen to you?" His mouth tightened.

"Yes. Please hear me out. You owe me that."

It was the wrong thing to say.

"I *owe* you that?" The air seemed to shimmer with his anger. "I don't owe you anything, Anya. Nothing at all."

It was the first time he'd said her name. It was said in rage, but still ...

She tugged at his arm. It was like tugging at a tree trunk. He could have been rooted to the earth for all the good it did her to tug. But ... this was her one chance. She'd waited ten years to say what needed to be said and she might not have another chance in this lifetime.

Certainly his body language didn't lead her to believe she could one day in the future call him up and invite him out for a coffee and talk. If he hadn't gotten over his anger in ten years, another ten years wouldn't do it.

Anya had seen up close and personal how long grudges could last. Generations. Centuries. She'd been in meeting rooms where talks almost came to blows over something that someone's great-great-uncle had done to someone else's great-great-uncle. Love was perishable. Rage? That could go on forever.

The idea of ending her days with Cal still hating her was unbearable. The weight of the idea sat on her chest like a boulder and made it hard to breathe.

Unending sadness for the rest of her days. *No, absolutely not.* This had to be cleared up, now.

"Sit down," she said, the words a command. Cal looked at her, startled. He'd known the happy young girl who'd never had any real problems to deal with. Who never raised her voice, because she never had to. Who never pushed, because she never had to.

Anya had done a lot of growing up in the meantime and she'd spent the past nine years at Peace and Jobs dealing with hard-headed men who had hated each other forever.

She had learned the hard way how to project power into her voice and she didn't need to raise it for it to work.

Cal sat.

Okay. Step one.

She didn't let go of his arm. He looked briefly down at her hand on his arm and she knew that he wanted to shake it off. She dug her fingers in.

Step two.

He wasn't going to shake her hand off him. He'd have to forcibly remove it and though this Cal was far from the boy she'd known, she didn't think it was in him to use force on a woman. Inside, he couldn't have changed that much.

He hadn't. He sat and faced her.

Step three.

He was staying put and was prepared to listen. She couldn't know how open minded he was but making people stay put and listen had been how she'd overcome a lot of obstacles in getting people who hated each other to agree on things.

Anya certainly didn't hate Cal but she wasn't too sure the opposite wasn't true. But she'd overcome impossible odds before.

She held his arm tightly. Unfortunately, she'd had to grab his left arm. The wrist was covered with a watch. A very nice one. A Patek Philippe, the kind that became an heirloom. If she'd been on his other side, she'd have grabbed his forearm and put her thumb on his wrist to gauge his physical reaction. Though right now his physical reaction was right beneath her palm. His muscles were rigid, unyielding. There was no give at all. He was rejecting her with everything in him.

Tough.

There was a structure to negotiations, going from low to high. Start asking for small things and work your way up. Two people who agreed that the sky was blue and water was wet could perhaps be brought to agree that peace was better than war.

But these weren't negotiations and Anya had to start from the top.

She took a deep breath.

"Do you remember that day in your room? When you told me about the scholarship to Stanford?"

"What?" He narrowed his eyes until there was only a golden glimmer between the lids. "What kind of trick question is that? Do I remember the day you left me? Fuck yes, I remember it."

She winced but he didn't seem to notice.

"You told me —"

"I told you I got that fellowship in Stanford and that I'd be moving to California. And I wanted you to move with me. I thought that was our plan. But it's one thing to fuck the guy who lives in your home town and who is convenient. It's quite another to follow that guy across the country and lose your cushy lifestyle."

Anya schooled her face to express nothing. She'd had long practice at it.

"That wasn't the way it was."

"Wasn't it?" Cal's voice was low and hard. He too had probably schooled himself not to show emotions but he couldn't control the red slash of anger staining his cheekbones. "It seemed to me it was. When I told you I got the scholarship you bounced out of my bed so fast it made my head spin. You left while my semen was still drying on your thighs. You couldn't wait to get out of there."

"No," she said steadily. "I didn't rush out, you are not remembering correctly. But it is true that I turned down your offer to follow you to California."

"For fuck's sake, Anya!" His voice rose and he leaned forward. "We'd talked about it, lots of times. You said you couldn't wait to leave Massachusetts and move to California! There was a period you put only Beach Boys on your phone. But then I guess you realized what life might be like with me, and without your father paying rent on your fancy apartment and without him slipping you a couple thou a month for incidentals. You'd have to live at my level and you just couldn't do it."

Part of that was true. She had been looking forward to the move. She'd wanted that move more badly than Cal. She couldn't wait. She loved her father but he'd become more and more heavy-handed, more controlling. It wasn't healthy. Moving across the country with the man she loved made more and more sense every day. She hadn't changed her mind. Her father had changed it for her.

"What my father gave me went straight into my savings account. And he insisted on the apartment because it had good security. You knew me. You *knew me!*" She stopped, throat vibrating with emotion. "You knew I didn't pull back because of the money."

"I thought I knew you." Cal was trying to stay cool but his breathing speeded up. "But I didn't. I didn't know you at all. Otherwise you couldn't have done what you did."

Anya opened her mouth, then closed it. What she was about to say she had never said to any human being on earth. Her father had gone to his grave and she'd never talked.

But it didn't make any difference now.

She kept her voice low. A trick a psychologist taught her. When emotional, pitch your voice low. Tension makes the vocal cords tighten and the voice rise. If you keep your voice low you can trick your vocal cords into not betraying tension or anxiety or fear. It was a trick that had served her well over the years, in the middle of shouting matches.

"That day —" he jerked his arm but she held onto it. He didn't want to hear about that day. Well, tough shit.

"A month before that day," she continued, "I spent the morning with my father. He called me to his office and said we had to talk. He didn't often do that. I was getting good grades, I was working hard, I didn't know what he wanted to say."

Actually, she'd thought he'd called her in for the eleven billionth time to ask her to ditch Cal, whom he hated.

"Called you in to ask you to get rid of me, I bet," Cal said sourly.

"It actually wasn't about you. It was about him. He was dying." She felt his muscles jerk. "You didn't know he was dead?"

"Sure, I knew." Cal's mouth twisted. "It was in all the papers the next year. Got a lot of press. Sudden heart attack of major industrialist. Pillar of the community. Gave tons of money to charity. Great tragedy for the community. The usual."

"It wasn't a heart attack and it wasn't sudden." Anya finally let go of his arm. For the moment, Cal wasn't going anywhere. He was intrigued enough to hear her out. That was all she needed. If he forgave her, that would be even better, but she wasn't holding out hope. No one knew better than her how the truth rarely set you free. "He had pancreatic cancer and the doctor had given him two months to live.

He actually lived for another six months. We needed every day of those six months."

"How so?" Cal asked the question reluctantly, as if the words were forced out of his mouth.

"You know I didn't have anything to do with Daddy's business. I was interested in international relations and languages. I thought everything was fine but when I went to him that morning, Daddy told me that the business was on the brink of bankruptcy."

She saw his eyes widen slightly.

"Yeah." She nodded. "I had no idea. He told me that morning. That the company was going under but that he might have found a buyer. Daddy wanted above all for the buyer to guarantee no job losses. It was part of the contract. That no one be fired for five years. He figured it was the best he could get. But that if the buyer thought Daddy was sick or incapacitated he'd be ruthless and simply buy cheap and lay off as many workers as he could. That's what some venture capital firms do. Buy up distressed businesses cheap, sell off the parts, fire all the workers. Some of daddy's employees had been with him for thirty years. He was sick at the thought of having to sell and then have massive layoffs."

Anya stopped, remembering that horrible day. Her father hadn't been an easy character and work had eaten up his life. They weren't close but she'd loved him. Just how much she loved him had hit her heart like a blow when he told her he had very little time left. Knowing how much he'd sacrificed to build the company, she also knew how much it hurt him to have to sell it, his life's work.

Cal was listening to her intently. "You mean you were with me knowing that your father was dying and that the family business was being sold?" His mouth tightened. "You knew that for a whole month?"

"Yes." The most horrible period of her life. She'd learned that she was going to lose her father and then she lost Cal.

His lips tightened, eyes faraway as he remembered that day. "You gave no sign. Nothing." There was dark accusation in his deep voice.

She sighed. "Dad made me swear to tell no one. He said the lives and livelihoods of thousands of people depended on keeping the situation secret. The people working for him and their families. I took an oath, Cal. I swore to him that I wouldn't tell anyone. That I wouldn't give any sign that anything was wrong. It broke my heart that I knew I wasn't going to be able to tell you anything. But ... I thought I was going to have time. That the deal would be signed soon and then I'd be able to talk. A month or two at the most and then I could tell you. But then —"

"Then I was awarded the fellowship."

"And I couldn't go with you." The words were pushed out of her tight throat. She could still remember the horror of realizing what she had to do. She had to leave Cal so he could go on to his destiny. Because she'd known, beyond a shadow of a doubt, that if she told Cal the truth, he'd have stayed by her side. And he would miss a once-in-a-lifetime opportunity.

She'd rather claw her own eyes out than have him sacrifice his life, his future, for her.

He spoke slowly. "Not if you had to stay by your father's side, no."

And once she'd understood what she had to do, she had to do it fast and brutally. He'd desperately tried to contact her and she'd avoided him. He didn't know that she'd cried for days in her apartment.

"No," she said softly.

Cal bowed his head, frowning. She knew that look, intimately. It was what she'd secretly called his dog-chewing-on-a-bone look, when he had a difficult problem to solve. He shook his head, once, as if trying to clear it.

When he lifted his head, the scowl was less fierce. "So —"

Two simultaneous opening bars from the original Star Trek show sounded.

"My phone," she said.

"My phone," he said.

Anya looked at him, startled, and opened her purse.

She'd been told that the principals of the Accords would be notified by text when the 'family photo' — the photo of historical record — was about to be taken.

She pulled out her phone — and froze, the text forgotten.

Cal froze too. They stared at each other's phones.

Their phones were both iphones, the exact same model — and their phone protectors both had the exact same image on the back.

Roj.

Peace, in Klingon.

They were both Star Trek nerds. Over that last summer, they'd taught themselves Klingon, in a little friendly rivalry. Anya had learned it better because she was a linguist, but Cal had studied hard and become semi-fluent. His first foreign language.

They'd had so much fun. She hadn't had fun like that since ... since Cal.

This time when tears sprang to her eyes, she couldn't blink them back. Separated by ten years, they'd bought the same phone and the same phone protector. That protector wasn't commercially available, Anya had had had it made to order. So had Cal, apparently. Her trembling hand covered her mouth and she didn't wipe the tears falling down her cheeks.

Time telescoped, collapsed, and it was as if she were back in the room with the boy she'd loved, and who'd loved her.

"Oh Cal," she whispered, throat aching. "I've missed you *so much.*"

He didn't answer. He simply held out his arms and she fell into them.

4

He was holding Anya in his arms again. *Anya.* It felt surreal. It felt perfect. She'd fallen into him and he just gathered her up and held her close while she wept violently. Her slender body shook with the sobs. He held her more and more tightly until he worried that he might be hurting her, but she held him just as tightly. As if she could burrow right through his suit and his skin until she was inside him.

Fuck yeah.

He placed his hands on her narrow back, feeling the convulsing muscles, the air rushing in and out of her lungs in huge gulps. Her own arms were around his chest, hands not meeting in the back. Years of working hands-on in desert desalination plants had whittled him down but had broadened his chest. She was leaning against him so hard, cheek pressed over his heart. He rested his chin on the top of her head — her hat actually — and just held her. Knowing she'd be both feeling and hearing the beat of his heart.

The heart that only beat for her. Had only ever beaten for her.

In that moment, Cal surrendered to the truth. He was holding in his arms the only woman he'd ever loved and ever would love.

The filmy lacy veil of her hat caught up in the buttons of his pleated dress shirt.

He moved his chin but the veil wrinkled up. He could shift it with his hand but that would mean letting go of her and he couldn't do it.

He looked down at her, short blue-black strands of hair framing her face. The color combination with her glowing blue eyes was striking.

Her sobs were dying down, just a little. She was crying for their lost love, for the lost years. For the days and nights they'd been apart. But ... she was in his arms *right now*. He wasn't dead and he wasn't lost to her. He was right here. She was crying for him but he was right ... here.

She took in a deep, shuddering breath and let it out on a sigh.

"You dyed your hair black," Cal said, touching the strands. He didn't care. She could dye her hair any color she wanted. Blue with pink stripes for all he cared.

"No." Her voice was waterlogged. He looked down and saw thick eyelashes, sharp cheekbones, a delicate chin. "Not dyed. It's a wig."

A wig?

Cal slid a hand up her back, the black beads clinking softly, until he reached the satiny skin of her neck. Looking down, he could see her delicate neck, the tiny knobs of her spine. But there was something wrong with her hair, it was too coarse. Anya's hair had always been soft and fine. Cal slid his fingers up her slender neck, kept going, reached under the weave and lifted away the wig of short black hair, together with the hat and the sexy little veil. He tossed the wig and the hat away, pulled out a few pins anchoring her hair and that soft golden blonde cascade fell over his hands in smooth perfumed waves.

Oh God.

He ran his hands over her scalp, then fanned out her hair so it covered her shoulders, fell down her back. It was a shorter than when he'd last seen her, but still glorious, still striking.

He lifted his head and so did she and they looked at each other.

Some trick in the acoustics of the ancient building made the notes of the quartet in the courtyard float up, bright silver notes, like a soundtrack made for Anya.

The whole room was a set designed to showcase her, like a pearl on velvet. Everything gleamed. The silver frames and decorative bowls, the chandeliers and crystal vases, the gold-flocked wallpaper, the frescoed ceiling. The most beautiful place Cal had ever seen and in it was the most beautiful woman Cal had ever known.

This was so familiar, Cal holding the silken strands of her hair in his hands, looking down at her beautiful face. The face was slimmer, cheekbones more defined. Light lines starred her eyes, bracketed her mouth, but they did nothing to detract from her beauty. It was now a woman's face, but she was even more beautiful than she'd been as a girl, if that was possible.

His heart thumped in his chest so hard he wondered if he was bruising it.

He and his team had come under attack by ISIS twice.

His security team was good and he'd become good not only with his hands but with weapons and they'd repelled the attacks. He'd kept his cool throughout both attacks.

He wasn't keeping his cool now.

It felt like he was flying apart in a million pieces. This had happened to him over and over again in his dreams. Anya, in his arms, then Anya walking away.

Every single time he lived through that moment of separation as if it were the first time, feeling like she'd reached into his chest and wrenched his heart right out of his rib cage, leaving him a broken and bloody husk. Every single goddamned time.

He'd wake up sweating and shaking as if from a nightmare, the pain of Anya leaving him fresh and acute, like an open wound. For the first couple of years he'd had to take sleeping aids to get through a night without The Dream. Anya walking away forever.

And here she was.

Anya, her hair a golden cloud around her head, looking up at him with a soft expression in her eyes. How many times had he dreamed this over the past ten years, only to wake up clutching empty air?

When they'd been together, his hands wrapped in her hair always led to sex and *wham!* Like a knee jerk reaction, he was suddenly hard as stone.

There was like a hot wind in his head, blowing hard, scouring all thoughts away. There was only Anya in his arms, only Anya in the whole goddamn world.

He rose and tugged at her hand. She stood, moving right into his arms. This. This was what had been missing all these years. Cal bent his head and kissed her. She tasted familiar yet different. Her mouth was sweet but all those years were like a river that had washed so much away. Their youth and their innocence.

She didn't taste like a girl, she tasted like a woman. He pulled her even more tightly against him and she fit perfectly. She was less soft, less curvy, more tightly muscled. Strong. Endlessly enticing.

Her arms were around his neck, pulling tight, as if he might break away from her.

No. Nope. Not going to happen.

He wasn't going to pull away from her, he wanted to be *inside* her. Oh God, the image of that in his empty head. A naked Anya and him, inside her.

Call put his hand under her skirt. It was silk, with heavy beads, which made a musical tinkling sound. They had a little sound track, their moans, the tinkling beads, heavy breathing.

Beneath the skirt Anya was wearing black silky stockings that were thigh-highs. Mmm. Between the lacy tops of the stockings and her panties was an expanse of silky skin over strong, slender thigh. Cal's hand followed the top of the stocking until he came to the center of her. When they'd been young, he'd touched her there thousands of times, but he'd been in the desert these past ten years. Literally and figuratively.

His hand cupped her and he could feel her heat, like a little furnace. He couldn't touch her flesh and right then all he could think about was touching her and entering her. But there was a barrier.

It took him a second to realize it was her panties. Man, they had to go. Right now.

Cal took his other hand away from her neck and slid it under that heavy skirt, hooking both thumbs under a piece of stretchy lace and pulling down. His mouth never left hers.

The panties were at mid thigh and she shimmied until they dropped to the ground and she stepped out of them. Under that silk and those tinkling beads she was naked.

His head was about to explode.

Cal picked her up and walked a couple of steps to that heavy table with the armchairs around it. He kicked one of the armchairs out of the way, slid her skirt up and set her down on the edge of the table. It didn't occur to him until later that if the table had been less massive and heavy, they might have fallen to the ground. Then and there, all he could think of was Anya, here, naked, on the table.

Cal held the back of her neck with one hand while lowering her to the shiny surface of the table and unzipping himself with the other. He was massively aroused. He couldn't remember ever being this hot and excited and fucking hard. His dick felt like a club hanging off the front of his body, like something alien.

But it knew exactly where it wanted to go. In her. In Anya.

Cal bent over Anya, settling between her thighs, smooth and slim and strong, and entered her with one thrust. He sighed heavily, lost inside her.

Anya lifted her legs, wrapping them around his hips and he lost all control, slamming into her over and over with the full power of his body. It was too violent, too intense and it was over almost immediately. He erupted inside her, shaking as he came and came and came.

He'd kept his face buried in her neck, so taken with being inside her that he couldn't even kiss her. Now he kept his face buried in her neck because he was ashamed.

Shocked and embarrassed at losing control like some randy kid.

It didn't matter that Anya had left him brutally, she didn't deserve this ... rutting. Like a wild animal.

He was still clutching her hips with the full force of his hands, and he had strong hands. It was entirely possible he was hurting her and that thought burned him, lashed him like a whip.

Cal could barely lift his head to look at her, sure what he'd see. Anger, disgust. Maybe she'd think she'd been right to leave him after all. And — maybe she'd be right about that.

Maybe he was unworthy of her, after all.

Cal was many things, but he wasn't a coward. He had to face her. Apologize. Then leave her, this chapter of his life forever over.

It hurt, but he did it. He pulled out, looking down at her, slim hips at the edge of the table, soft ash-brown cloud of hair wet with her juices and his. As he pulled back, her legs fell to the floor and he saw red spots on her hips where his fingers had gripped tightly. Tomorrow she'd have bruises.

Oh, fuck.

5

Anya clutched the sides of the table, shaking.

Cal was on her, *in* her. She could hear his heavy breathing, as if he'd run ten miles. She found it hard to breathe too, but more because his full weight was on her, crushing her. She remembered exactly what Cal felt like on top of her. He was leaner now but he seemed to be more muscled and he was heavy as hell. She had to consciously expand her lungs to breathe and it wasn't easy.

Still, she wasn't agitating to have him get off of her. She liked it, liked that heavy weight anchoring her. She'd always felt that way. With Cal near her, nothing bad could happen.

Or so she'd thought. Plenty of bad things had happened.

But she also didn't want him to move off because for these few moments, she didn't have to face him. There was an undercurrent of anger in him, his love making had been rough. Cal had never been rough with her, ever, but just now there'd been strength and desire but not tenderness.

What would be on his face when he got off her and she opened her eyes? Did she really want to know?

Because she knew what would be on her face — longing. Love. Love that had never died. But if the same things weren't on his face, it would collapse her world.

All these years there'd been a little flame of hope in her heart. Tiny, but there. That maybe ... maybe his marriage would break up. And that afterward ... maybe he would come find her, lay his heart at her feet. Tell her he'd never stopped loving her.

It was a tiny spark of hope that no one knew about but which in the darkest, loneliest nights kept her warm. But even that spark of hope failed her, often. Working endlessly long days in dusty hotel meeting rooms in the Middle East, soaking up hostility on two, three, even four sides, falling exhausted into bed after midnight only to stare up at the ceiling, at times she'd lost hope that Cal could ever be in her life again. That things could ever be good again. That she'd know love again.

But here they were.

His marriage had broken up, and he'd found her. That part had come true. And they'd had sex — but it had been rough, even angry.

If there was no love there, not a tiny bit of love left for her in his heart, it would shatter her beyond repair. The pieces would never be put back together again. All hope would be gone. She'd have lost Cal, forever, even though he was right here.

Cal stood up, stood back. That heavy weight gone wasn't a good thing. She felt unmoored, something that had anchored her suddenly gone.

Anya slid off the table and stood up slowly, creakily. As if she'd suddenly aged a million years.

Cal was zipping himself up and when he was done he

looked exactly as he had before — like a tough, rich businessman, completely pulled together. Whereas she was sure
she looked like a wild woman — hair tousled around her
shoulders, lipstick smudged, dress askew. She moved and
felt something underfoot and looked down. Her underpants
— a black lace symbol of wantonness there on the parquet
floor.

She'd never ever felt dirty after they'd made love when
they were young. She'd always felt so exhilarated and happy
— as if touched by some sun god. Young and happy and so
in love.

Cal had always had this look on his face and she thought
it was his regular expression — bursting with joy, soft and
tender. Well, it wasn't his regular post-sex expression
anymore because he didn't have it now.

Not at all.

His face — so lean and dark — was taut and still,
completely closed to her. Those light brown eyes were
expressionless. She now understood in full that the Cal of
her memory was gone, essentially dead. This new man was
someone she didn't know, and now might never know.

For the first time, Anya felt awkward in his presence, that
same awkwardness she'd felt with most of the men she'd
been working with these past nine years. But most of those
men had been hostile to her plans and to the plans of Peace
and Jobs. They'd had no reason to be friendly to her and she
hadn't expected it.

Just as, apparently, she couldn't expect Cal to be friendly
to her.

She had to swallow that bitterness down.

Her hands twisted in front of her because she didn't
know what to do with them. Her palms itched to touch him,

her arms felt empty because she wanted to embrace him, yet couldn't.

With pain and sorrow she put herself into work mode — a frame of mind where her own feelings had no place, no value. It was all about the transaction.

"So," she said softly, watching his eyes.

"So." His tone was as hard as his expression.

They'd just made love — had sex, she corrected herself — but it was as if they were two strangers. She could smell the sex they'd had. She could feel her sex a little sore, their juices wet between her legs.

They hadn't taken precautions. She couldn't even think of that as her heart cracked a little. Cal was right in front of her, something she'd dreamed of for ten years. And yet it was as if he were a million miles away from her.

"I guess —" Anya stopped. Her brain was empty. She had no idea what she'd been about to say. All she knew was that she didn't want him to walk away from her with this cold, hard distance between them, with the memory of angry sex rippling in the air. She should say something, but what? Words lodged in her throat like stones, unable to come out, unable to stay inside her.

"What?" Cal stepped forward a little, but she didn't step back. Her head tilted back to watch his face. He was taller than she remembered. "What, Anya? You guess what?"

"I don't know," she whispered, miserably.

He was scowling ferociously now. "You don't know? *You don't know?* You sure as hell knew ten years ago. You had no trouble at all making yourself crystal clear that you didn't want me. So what is this? What just happened?" His long finger tapped her chest then his. "We just had sex. That's something, isn't it? Or did it mean as little to you now as it did then. I remember you got up out of our bed and left me without a care in the world."

She'd wept bitterly for days afterward.

"No." Her throat was so tight the word hurt. "Not without a care in the world."

Cal's jaw muscles worked as if he were biting something. "Sure as hell looked like that to me."

"I explained —"

"You explained *nothing*." The words exploded out of him. "What did you explain? That your dad was sick and was having economic problems and you thought — what? What did you think? That I'd blab that to the world? That I'd go around talking about a downturn at Voronov Industries? I didn't like him and he didn't like me but what the fuck, Anya. You didn't trust me enough to think I could keep my mouth shut? I wondered for ten freaking *years* what happened and this is worse than anything I could have imagined. You broke us up because you thought I'd *talk*?"

Oh god. She'd thought her heart would break ten years ago but this was a million times worse. It felt like she could hear her heart crack open.

"No." Damn, her entire chest hurt. It hurt to breathe. "No, I wasn't afraid you would talk. I knew you wouldn't. You were so honorable, you'd never do that."

Cal huffed out a harsh breath and turned around, putting his hands on his head. When he'd had long hair, he'd pull at it when he was frustrated. But it was cut military short now.

She stared at his broad back, shoulders stiff with anger. At her. She'd never seen him angry at her before. It was horrible.

"Goddammit, Anya!" he turned back to her. "Then what?

What the hell did you leave me for, like that, if you knew I'd keep my mouth shut? You knew that whatever it was you had to do, I'd stick by you."

"Oh yes." Her voice was soft. "Oh yes, I knew that."

His eyes burned, mouth tight. White lines of stress bracketed his mouth. "Then *why?*"

"Precisely because you'd stick by me."

He reacted as if she'd slapped him. "What?" His shoulders tightened, big hands fisting. "What kind of answer is that?"

Anya drew in a deep breath. She felt hollowed out, almost insubstantial. As if she were an empty vessel held together by will and skin. Deep inside she trembled, reaching out with a hand to grasp the edge of the table, hoping he wouldn't notice.

He did, of course. He'd always been so observant, her Cal. When she had her head in the clouds, Cal was always keenly aware of their surroundings.

It was like being naked again, him seeing inside her.

Deliberately, Anya looked at Cal, from his expensively barbered hair to the tips of his shiny dress shoes. She'd learned to monetize in her job, as a way to categorize. Cal was wearing at least ten thousand dollars, from his black Armani or Gucci tux to the Patek Philippe on his wrist.

"Look at you," she said, sweeping her hand to indicate him head to toe.

Startled, Cal looked down at himself.

"Is that an Armani you're wearing?"

He frowned. "Gucci."

My, all those years in war-torn cities, walking through rubble, sleeping on cots. She'd lost her touch. She used to be able to tell an Armani from a Gucci at a hundred paces.

"Even better. The last time I saw you, you were wearing torn jeans and a ratty tee shirt."

"The last time you saw me I was naked," he said, voice clipped.

She broke with his gaze and looked away. Ashamed and hurt. Wondering what the hell she was trying to do here. But then thought — *no. He needs to hear this.* "True. But you'd been wearing torn jeans and a tee that had been washed a thousand times before you got naked. And the jeans weren't bought distressed. They were worn right through at the knees."

"I was poor," he said curtly. "So what? What's your point?"

God yes, he'd been poor. He'd held down two jobs while studying full time and had accumulated massive student debt on top of it, yet he always insisted on paying whenever they went out. She had a generous allowance from her father but he wouldn't hear of her paying, not even for a coffee. Sometimes the only way she could get around that was to simply show up at his apartment with takeout. And she always made sure she brought more than they could eat so he'd have leftovers for a couple of days.

"Yes, you were very poor and your prospects at Boston U weren't good. You knew that as well as I did. You would continue working as a teaching adjunct and you'd have stayed there for at least another ten years, overworked and underpaid. The teaching jobs would have kept you so busy you wouldn't have been able to do any decent research. By the time you woke up ten years later, your career would've been gone, you'd have been living in genteel poverty and above all, you wouldn't have been able to hold down any jobs outside the university system. And even there, even brilliant as you are, you'd have had to hold tight to the ladder because younger, fresher, richer kids were coming right up behind you."

Cal's mouth tightened. He recognized what she was saying as true. It was all true.

"Your one big hope was that fellowship in Stanford, and the job at Benson Labs. It was your big break. And look at you." She waved her hand at him again, top to bottom. "You own *Phoenix*, one of the biggest engineering companies on earth. I was involved in the Diplomacy Dossier so I didn't pay much attention to the Tech Dossier, but even I have heard of Phoenix. It's a big part of what makes the Accords work. Cheap water. Solving the age-old problem of potable water forever. It's a miracle of engineering and it's probably the biggest engineering contract on earth and it's all your doing. I cannot imagine how hard you've worked to create the technology and build your company but I know that you deserve it all. I heard talk at one point of a Nobel Peace Prize for the owner of Phoenix. I had no idea that was you."

Cal's face hadn't softened but he shrugged one big shoulder. "So it was an opportunity, so what? You knew that. You're the one who encouraged me to try out for that post-doc fellowship program, remember?"

"I do." Anya nodded. Cal had deserved so much more than his future would have been back in Boston. "And I was more than willing to go to California with you."

"Until you weren't," Cal said bitterly.

How hard those days had been, after her father had told her of his illness, of the possibility of his company going belly up taking two thousand jobs with it. Thousands of employees and their families that counted on the business. She was making it work, keeping it together. Cal had had no idea of her stress, which is how she'd wanted it. There was the hope that the sale could go through before he was offered anything.

And then he'd won the fellowship and her heart had broken. She knew what she had to do and she did it.

Cal placed a big hand on the back of his neck and looked away, maybe at that scene ten years in the past where their lives were irrevocably shattered. "I can't believe you didn't tell me. I can't believe you thought I'd talk, that I could jeopardize the sale of your father's company."

"Oh no." Anya reached out a hand, hesitated a moment, then touched his forearm. It was hard as steel and she could feel the tension under her fingertips. So strange — they'd had sex and yet this light touch felt more intimate than the sex. Intimate and dangerous. "I told you, I didn't think you'd talk. I knew you better than that. You're an honorable person."

Cal looked up at the ceiling and blew out a breath. "Then what the fuck, Anya! What made you —" his voice cracked.

She reached up, gently took his chin and made him look at her. She waited a minute so he would *look*. Look beyond his anger and hurt.

"I was hoping I could ... run out the clock. That Dad could sell the company under his conditions, that we could save all those jobs at least for five years. I knew Dad wouldn't last long, but he'd lived a long life under his terms. He missed my mother terribly. He was ready to go. Another few months and at least his dream of saving his employees' jobs would come true. But then—you got the Stanford offer and ..." Her throat closed up. Simply seized up. She couldn't get anything out, it felt like thorns had grown inside her throat. It hurt to talk, it hurt to breathe.

Cal was scowling at her, but she had to do this. "And I had to give you up."

The cords of his neck stood out. "Goddamit Anya, *why?* Why didn't you tell me what was happening?"

"Because you'd have turned the offer down," she said simply and watched as the anger spilled out of him, like air out of a balloon. "I know you. If I told you I was having problems, and couldn't come with you, you'd have said no to Stanford." Again, she waved a hand at him, at the highly successful man he'd become, so very different from the harried academic he would have been, a shadow of what he could have been. All that potential — gone. He'd have done that for her without a second thought. And she'd have never forgiven herself.

Cal shoved his hands in his tuxedo pants pockets, mouth tight.

"You know I'm right, Cal," she said softly, keeping her gaze on his face.

He'd once been an open book to her. He'd been just a boy then and now he was a man. A man who'd founded a global enterprise, had fought his way up. But for just an instant there, a fleeting second, she saw the boy she'd loved so much.

"Think back, to ten years ago. Think back to —" She swallowed heavily. "— to what we meant to each other. And imagine I come to you and say I have a terrible problem to face, that I have to shield my father while negotiating a favorable sale of the company, otherwise the lives of thousands of people will be wrecked. That I am under terrible, soul-crushing pressure. What would you have said?"

He stood silently.

"What would you have done? I can't even to begin to

imagine you saying, 'Sorry babe. That's on you, not on me. Not my problem. I have the opportunity of a lifetime and I'm not missing it.' Not in my wildest imagination. You would have been incapable of leaving me if you'd thought I was in trouble. Am I right?" He still didn't say anything, though his jaw clenched. She took a step closer to him. "*Am I right?*"

He nodded, a jerk of his head. Not wanting to admit it.

"You were young and in love and so sure of yourself. No way you'd have abandoned me. You couldn't see the future, but I could. Very well. You beat incredible odds getting as far as you had, but you were at the end of the road where you were. That PhD wasn't going to get you much further if you wanted to stay in Boston with me. They were already loading you down with TA jobs and editing scientific papers and having you all but sweeping the floors of the labs. There wasn't a big project for you to join. You'd have been stuck there forever and maybe not even unhappy, but you wouldn't have reached your full potential. You certainly wouldn't have been what you are now. The head of Phoenix, a man who changed the world. I don't know much about the Technical Dossier. The Diplomatic Dossier was hard enough. But even I know that without cheap water, the Accords would never have taken place. You did that, Cal. You're right up there with Gates and Jobs and it never would have happened without that fellowship at Stanford. I could see it then, plain as day, how far you'd get. And you couldn't see it. The only way to get you to go was to push you away."

The memory of that sharp, unending pain nearly brought her to her knees. That afternoon she'd felt as if she were cutting her own heart right out of her chest. She'd thought they had time, but no. She'd had to devastate the man she loved and destroy her own heart in the process. Her throat was sore, the words coming out as if cut by knives. "So that's what I did."

"Jesus, Anya." He was pale, features tight, lines bracketing his mouth. "I can't believe you did that. I can't believe you didn't come to me at least after the sale. I remember reading about it later the next year. Why didn't you come to me then, explain everything?"

"I did," she said softly.

Oh God, she'd thought of him every single day. Because she wanted to touch him, hold him, she groped for something else to hold. Her cell. She picked it up from the top of the piano, clutched it, the very symbol of how in tune they were, always had been, probably always would be. But she wanted to hold him, not the cell, so she put it back down.

"*What?*"

"I did come to you. We made the sale, the jobs were saved, and my father died. After I buried him, that very same day, I flew out to California, hired a car and drove to Palo Alto. I didn't even look you up before leaving. All I could think about was being free of obligations and making my way back to you. It was evening when I arrived, dark, but I was in a frenzy to see you. I drove around while trying to book a hotel room on the phone — there was some kind of conference and everything was full — and then I saw you."

He breathed out. "When was this?"

"End of July."

"Shit."

She closed her eyes, remembering. "Yeah. I was waiting for a traffic light to turn green when I saw you with this beautiful woman. The two of you crossed the street right in front of me. You were arm in arm. She had a huge rock on her left-hand ring finger. That wasn't so bad. But you had a gold wedding band."

He blew out a gusty breath. "I met Martina in April and we were married a couple of months later."

Didn't take you long to forget me, she thought, but didn't say. She didn't have any right to snark or anger. But if she thought her heart had broken back in Boston when she left him, that was nothing. Watching Cal cross the street right in front of her in Palo Alto, arm in arm with a beautiful woman, the two of them laughing and staring into each other's eyes, the very picture of two people in love — well that had made her heart implode in her chest.

"I looked you up, then, finally. Should have done that before jumping on to a plane. And there it was, the wedding announcement. I looked at it then looked up at the two of you crossing the street."

It still hurt, ten years later. Watching Cal and his new bride

cross the street, walk down the opposite sidewalk to a fancy restaurant, watching him open the door for his bride with that protective aura she had thought was for her and her alone ... it had been such a shock that she'd had to pull over on the next street and wait for her hands to stop shaking. She couldn't drive in that moment, it was like she'd been concussed, only in the heart.

It had hurt to breathe.

She couldn't stay the night in Palo Alto, simply couldn't. So she turned around and drove back to SFO and waited on a hard, uncomfortable chair all night for the early flight back to Boston, staring into space, feeling each slow, painful beat of her heart.

Cal watched her, those light eyes almost glowing. "We married in June and were divorced by November."

Anya let out a breath she didn't know she was holding. "What went wrong?"

He shrugged a broad shoulder. "She wasn't you. She looked like you, a little. But she wasn't you."

There was nothing to say to that.

"You made us lose ten years." His voice was hard, jaw muscles working.

There was nothing to say to that, either. Except she had to try. Watching him carefully, speaking as if her words were so volatile they could spark an explosion, she said, "We did lose the last ten years. But —" Anya carefully gathered her courage, feeling as if she were leaning out over a huge precipice, about to fall into an abyss. "But maybe not the next ten years."

She blinked back tears. It wasn't the moment for tears. And she thought she'd cried herself out years ago.

The thin tendril of hope hung out there, quivering and trembling. It could be severed by a sharp word or shake of the head.

But still ... The words were out there in the world.

Maybe not the next ten years.

Cal didn't say anything, anything at all. Every moment somehow gave the words more weight and heft. They were taking on a life of their own.

Anya felt hollowed out, almost devastated with hope. This was crazy. Any second Cal was going to turn his back, walk out the door and carry the rest of her life away with him. He was angry and he had every right to be angry. She'd hurt him, badly. She hadn't wanted to, but she had. And if there were a time machine to take her back to that terrible moment in time, she'd do it again. Cal had deserved his moment in the sun. He'd earned everything that had come to him. No way she'd take it away.

The words were still there, a possibility shimmering in the air. *Maybe not the next ten years.*

The lights flickered once, twice.

Or was it her heart?

Say something, Cal. The words were right there, she could taste them in her mouth. But she also didn't want him to say anything. Like that scientific paradox Cal told her about — Schrodinger's Cat. Until you opened the box, you didn't know if the cat was dead or alive.

Until Cal spoke, she didn't know whether to hope or not.

"The next ten years," he said, voice flat and low.

Tension gripped her throat. She couldn't say anything, no words would come out. All she could do was nod.

"Hmm." A corner of his mouth went up. "I like the sound of that."

Was that — was that a smile? Then she ran through what he'd said. He liked the sound of the next ten years.

A raw sound came from her throat. Not a sob. More like her heart trying to fight its way out of her throat. She fell into his arms, crying wildly. She'd just finished crying and here she was again. She never cried, but now it was like her eyes were created to leak water.

Her arms went around his waist and she leaned into him, just like she used to. And just like before, his arms went around her in a tight embrace. She felt safe, protected. She hadn't felt protected like this for ten years. He didn't try to shush her, he just bent his head over hers and cupped the back of her head and let her cry. She felt a kiss on the top of her head and cried harder.

Oh God, this felt so good! She'd missed this, missed this so fiercely. And now — now he was back. The Cal she'd loved so much.

Anya shifted her head and kissed him right over his heart. Right on a very expensive Egyptian cotton pleated tuxedo shirt, leaving a lipstick kiss.

She laughed, voice soggy. "I left lipstick stains on your shirt."

"Do I look like I care?" She felt the vibration of his deep voice against her cheek resting on his chest and sighed happily.

His firm fingers on her chin lifted her face to his. His face was — oh God. *Yes.* This was Cal, her Cal, come back to life. He looked like he'd dropped decades and he was smiling.

"Anya," he murmured and kissed her. She opened her mouth and her heart to him, kissing him back and —

The lights went out.

It took her a second to realize that the lights had blacked out and that it wasn't she who'd blacked out.

There was a snick of the door opening, but the lights must have been out all over the villa because there was no light coming from the hall. There was just a tenuous glow from the torches flickering in the corners outside.

The music had stopped, voices rising in surprise and consternation.

And suddenly there were shadows darker than the darkness. Hard hands yanked her away. The sounds of meaty thuds, a cry of pain from a male voice that wasn't Cal's. Another thud, the crash of wood breaking. The hard hands holding her tightened as she tried to break away. There was a struggle going on, dark and deadly, grunts of violence, the heavy breathing of combat, the sounds of flesh striking flesh.

Cal was fighting. He was a good fighter, had been a martial arts adept all his life.

Had these men come to kidnap him? If so, he was giving them the fight of their lives.

Anya stopped struggling and didn't make a sound. The last thing Cal needed was to be distracted by her, by her voice, by fear for her.

She couldn't help him in any way but by her stillness and silence so she was still and silent.

A body flew across the room, landing against what she remembered was a console with an antique mirror above it. She felt the rush of air as the body flew past. The mirror fell in crystalline shards that tinkled as they fell to the floor, a macabre contrast to the sounds of violence.

Could that body have been Cal? Was he now lying in a pool of blood from a thousand cuts?

No, the animal-like sounds of close battle continued. A fist connected with a stomach, breath leaving a body with a pained whoosh. A sudden *crack* of a bone breaking.

A low, male voice said something in Chinese. *The spray.* What —

The sound of liquid spraying, the sound of a body thudding heavily to the floor.

Someone switched on a flashlight with a narrow beam set on low. But it was enough to get a dim perception of the situation.

There were two men standing, other than the one gripping her from behind, plus two men on the ground, very still. One of them was Cal and her heart nearly stopped.

The two men standing had pushed up goggles onto their foreheads. Night vision goggles. These sons of bitches had had night vision! Not only had they outnumbered Cal five to one — they'd been able to see while he was fighting blind.

And now Cal was motionless on the ground, as if asleep or ... no. She wasn't going there. Cal couldn't be dead, simply couldn't. The narrow beam of the flashlight cast him in pitiless shades of light and darkness but she couldn't see a pool of blood around him.

Maybe ...

Yes!

His broad chest was slowly rising and falling! Oh God! Anya put a hand to her mouth to suppress a sob of relief. The less attention she drew to herself the better. But now that she knew Cal was alive, a rush of rage bolted through her.

The door to the hallway opened. The sounds of panic from downstairs — shouts and cries — flowed in. The light from the torches outside was faint, just enough to see by.

A tall man slipped into the room, this man dressed in a costume. She couldn't make out exactly what the costume was. For the first time, Anya realized that the five attackers were dressed as soldiers. Not in uniform, but as commandos.

So ... was the man dressed in a costume an outsider? One of the members of the Accords team who'd heard the sounds of combat? Someone who would help her?

She opened her mouth to scream, but the man holding her wrapped one arm tightly around her shoulders and put a big hand against her mouth. Then, horribly, his thumb and index finger pinched her nostrils, cutting off her air.

Her brain blanked as the animal instinct to survive made her writhe, kicking him, scratching at his arms. But her pretty 1920s-style shoes weren't meant to hurt and his arms were covered in some kind of material that was impervious to her scratches.

She struggled violently, scrabbling to hurt him in any way she could, writhing in his hold. She was strong, but he was stronger.

And the physical efforts were using up all her oxygen. Her lungs tried to pull in air, uselessly, and she could feel herself start to lose consciousness. Her struggles stopped.

"Settle down," the man dressed in a costume said irritably. "Stop it."

As if that were a cue, the hand covering her mouth and nose lifted and she gasped in air greedily in huge gulps, the animal part of her rejoicing in the fact that she wasn't going to die right now.

One man was holding up a cellphone with the flashlight function on, studying the bodies on the floor.

Tears swam in her eyes as she studied Cal slumped on the parquet flooring. Still, she could see that massive chest rising and falling.

A sob escaped her and she thanked whoever was up there that he'd survived the attack.

But now that the clouds of adrenaline and oxygen deprivation were clearing, she realized that of course he'd be alive. This was a kidnapping. They'd come for Cal, maybe not realizing that he could fend off attacks. The two men on the floor attested to that fact.

Cal had gone down fighting.

Good for him, she thought viciously. She hoped that the two men on the floor were dead, or at least maimed. Whoever they were, they intended Cal harm and she focused her hatred on them, and on the man holding her.

The light from the cellphone's flashlight function

panned the room and she got a better look at the man who'd slipped in after the fight. Unlike the others, he was dressed in costume, some kind of 17th-century version of a soldier, like a musketeer. He wore thigh high boots and a freaking sword at his side. And he wasn't here to help her. The body language of the attackers made that clear. He was in on the kidnapping.

Anya's eyes narrowed as she tried to memorize his face in the almost impossibly dim light. The others had balaclavas over their faces but this man just had a black masquerade mask around the eyes.

The light was low, but there was something half familiar about the figure, even with the masquerade mask. She knew she'd seen him somewhere before. If she could, she would identify him, testify against him and take him down.

The man looked around without a word, taking in the bodies on the floor and Anya, immobilized by the big man behind her. "You know what to do," he said to the man holding her and slipped back out the door. The voice was American.

Anya expected the men to pull up Cal's deadweight body and spirit him away but they just left him there on the ancient parquet floor. Why weren't they picking him up? They were here to kidnap him, clearly. She hadn't really thought it through but the owner of Phoenix must be a very rich man.

The part of the world where she and Cal had been working these past years, kidnapping for ransom was almost a sector of the economy.

These sons of bitches were going to hold Cal to ransom. No telling what his executives would be willing to pay to get him back. The company was one of the largest in the world.

Though Cal had gone to extremes to not appear in the lime-light, these guys knew who they were kidnapping.

Anya stayed as quiet and still as possible. They wouldn't forget about her — these guys were pros — but maybe she could convince them she was harmless.

She wasn't. The instant they were gone with Cal, she'd raise pure hell with the authorities. She had some clout as deputy director for Peace and Jobs and her boss was sure to help her. The kidnapping of the head of Phoenix was a big deal, endangering the Accords themselves. Every single power lever she could invoke would crank into action.

One of the men rushed past her and stirred the air. There was a faint sickly sweet odor she recognized immediately. Chloroform. She'd been in a refugee camp that had been attacked by terrorists who felt threatened by the Accords and they'd run out of morphine and had had to use chloroform until medics could arrive. She'd never forget the smell.

That was how they had subdued Cal. She knew him, knew his expertise. She remembered with a rush of warmth the depth of the strength of the muscles she'd caressed not half an hour ago. Only putting him out allowed them to take him.

The fucking cowards. Without thinking, she made to move toward Cal and was stopped by a punch to the stomach. Anya doubled over, all the breath in her body gone. For a horrible second she thought she'd suffocate but finally she was able to wheeze in a breath, two.

The man who'd punched her turned her around and Anya stiffened. The light was behind him, his face in dark shadow, ski mask in place. He took a step forward as her heart plummeted.

She was a witness. Were they going to kill her?

Anya opened her mouth to say that she hadn't seen anyone's face, they could rest assured she couldn't identify them, when the man said, "Anya Voronova."

She blinked, stunned.

The balaclava covered his features, disguising them. Only the eyes, cold, dark and unfeeling, were visible.

"Do you have your phone?" he asked.

She couldn't answer, merely staring at him.

"Do you have your phone?" he repeated impatiently. His English was almost perfect, but he was foreign.

Anya reached out, grabbed her phone on the top of the piano. "Y-yes."

"Put this on." Crazily, he held out a Venetian porcelain mask, only it didn't have holes for eyes. The eyes were painted on, but so realistically that you had to look closely to see that.

She felt numb. "What?"

The eyes grew colder. "You heard me. Don't make me say it twice."

She fit the mask onto her face with trembling fingers, tying the tapes behind her head, effectively blinding herself. They didn't want her to see anything while they abducted Cal. But if they left her alive, she'd sound the alarm immediately.

Then she felt something like a rod against her side.

"That's a gun," the voice said coldly. "And it's got hollow point ammo. It will expand inside you until your insides are pulped. Do you understand me?"

Anya froze. "Yes."

"Yes what?"

"Yes I understand you." And she did.

"We're going to walk out of here. I'm going to have my arm around you as if we were lovers, so follow my lead. If you try to say anything to anyone, I'll shoot. Are we clear?"

She nodded jerkily.

"Then let's go." An arm fell around her shoulders but the rod at her side — the gun — was still there. He directed her toward the door. She didn't hear the door open but she knew it had by the burst of sounds of panic from downstairs coming up the stairwell.

Apparently the lights were still out.

The noise was so loud that even if she could scream for help, no one would hear her. And she was blind, had no idea if there was anyone on this floor who could help her.

The man who could save her was behind her, lying unconscious.

She stumbled blindly forward under the impetus of her captor's arm.

How could she have been so wrong? They weren't here to kidnap Cal.

They were here for her.

6

His head hurt. His chest hurt. His legs hurt. His fucking toenails hurt. But most of all his head. The pain intensified with every beat of his heart.

What the fuck?

Cal lifted his head, was instantly sorry and let it thunk back to the ground when the world whirled around him in jerky spasms. Massive pain and nausea. It was even more horrible because he was in the dark. If he'd been able to see, he knew he'd have seen the ceiling spinning around sickeningly. It was even more awful in the darkness.

He lay still, trying to understand what was happening. He'd once fallen unconscious out in the desert, so engrossed in solving a pipeline problem he hadn't noticed that he was badly dehydrated. But when he regained consciousness, he knew exactly where he was and what he needed. Water.

This time he didn't have a clue where he was, what he was doing on the floor in pitch blackness.

Lights flickered, just long enough for him to see where he was. In a fancy historic room. As the lights flickered again memory flickered too. He was in ... Venice. Venice? That felt right. In Palazzo ... Maltese.

The insides of his stomach threatened to come right up and he swallowed heavily, pushing the bitter bile back down. He breathed the nausea and dizziness away.

The lights came on and he opened his eyes. He was on a beautiful honey-colored parquet floor, the tiles so small it was almost a mosaic. The room was elaborate, the ceiling frescoed. Casting his eyes to the ceiling almost made him throw up. God, what was this nausea about? Did he have food poisoning? Like that time in Yemen when he'd puked his guts out for four days?

He consulted his stomach. There wasn't anything there. He hurt everywhere else but not his stomach.

So what was going on?

He was at eye level with the floor and saw something nearby. Something small and shiny and black. He reached out, scrabbled on the shiny wooden floor for an instant and brought it back to scrutinize it.

A bead. A black bead. He frowned. There were several of them just like it scattered over the floor. What the —

And it all came rushing back. Lights going out. Men rushing through the door, fighting them. Some liquid sprayed in his face as Anya was being brutally manhandled.

Anya!

Cal put a hand on the floor and lifted his torso, waiting impatiently, eyes closed, for the extreme dizziness to die down. He hated waiting, but he had to, otherwise he'd fall down. He couldn't afford to fall down — he needed to get to Anya as fast as humanly possible.

Another hand on the floor.

One leg under him. Other leg. Everything trembling. The world spinning.

Fuck this.

He stood up, shooting out a hand to clutch the edge of the large table for balance. The table where he and Anya had made love.

Anya.

She'd been taken.

That thought was part of the world spinning because he couldn't seem to make it work in his head. If anything, they should have come for *him*. Cal had survived two kidnapping attempts. He was worth a lot of money and not only would his company pay, but the organizing body of the Mediterranean Accords would pay. He travelled with a security entourage except for right now, this evening, in the heart of the West, celebrating the future.

Shit.

There were two men on the floor and he could just barely recall the fight to put them down. They'd been good but he'd been better and he was fighting with Anya in the room, in danger. He'd have faced an army if he'd had to.

The two men were breathing, which he was sorry about. Had they somehow gotten the better of him, knocked him out? No. His head hurt but not from a blow. His head hurt from the inside. He'd been ... gassed? Cal sniffed the air, a sickeningly sweetish scent barely perceptible. Chloroform. Fuckers had put him out, gassed him, with chloroform.

Cal knelt slowly next to one of the bodies, hoping he wouldn't pass out. He didn't, but it was touch and go and he felt a billion years old as he put a knee to the floor.

Both men were dressed tactically in black, the material Nomex, he discovered when he touched it. He rapped his knuckles against the chest of the closest man. His knuckles made a pocking sound. Body armor. Balaclavas and tiny goggles, which he recognized as the very latest iteration of night vision. Only special forces had them, or so he thought. Or maybe these were special forces, which was a terrifying thought.

Specops soldiers out for Anya. Specops in any country trained ruthlessly for years to kill and maim. And they had Anya. He breathed down the horror of that thought.

Who were these men? He pulled off the goggles and balaclava of both men. They had an Asian cast to their features. Cal didn't know what they were — Chinese, Japanese. Maybe something else. There were no identifying marks on the combat gear and even if they were, he wouldn't have been able to tell Chinese script from Japanese script. Anya could — she knew Chinese well.

He checked their pockets — nothing. They were unarmed, or at least had no firearms on them. Italy was a country where firearms weren't permitted. No weapons at all, not even a knife. That meant something. Probably that they didn't want blood stains to show that violence had been done.

Cal looked around the room. Somehow no furniture had been broken. One mirror had shattered, but with the lights out, that could have been an accident.

Digging through the pockets of one of the men, Cal brought out something that made his blood boil. A length of rope. *They intended to tie Anya up?* Those motherfuckers wanted to tie her?

They both had a piece of rope in their gear. Okay. Cal was more than willing to use that against them. He tied the men's hands behind their backs, pulling the rope extra tight, and tied each man to a leg of the heavy table in the center of the room. When they gained consciousness, they weren't going anywhere.

When he stood up, he had to put a hand out to steady himself while the room twirled crazily.

He stood for another minute, living with the extreme dizziness, and despaired at the thought of Anya somehow gone. Somehow *captured*. Anya, in the hands of enemies.

Did someone figure out what Anya meant to him? She'd been kidnapped to extort money from him, was that it? Well, it worked, that was for damned sure. He'd pay anything, anything at all, to keep her safe, get her back. He'd gut Phoenix. A company could be refounded, but he would never find another Anya. He knew, because he'd already tried.

However, Anya was important in her own right, not just important to him. Was she kidnapped because of something she knew? Kidnapping her at this late date wouldn't do anything to slow the Accords, though. They were in hand, there wasn't much that could stop the juggernaut. And though Peace and Jobs was an important organization, it was important morally, not financially or even politically.

Cal straightened. He still felt dizzy but not so dizzy he couldn't see straight. His head hurt but pain was nothing. He could ignore pain, he'd done it before.

They'd taken Anya, the thought nearly brought him to his knees again. He couldn't afford that. He needed to find her, fast, and he needed help.

Cal picked up his cell and prepared to press his index finger to the screen to unlock it and punch in his code — Anya's birthday. But the screensaver wasn't his. His screensaver was a photo he'd taken one day at dawn of the great palace in Petra known as the Treasury, the colors pale pink and light blue. This cell's screensaver was a photo of Petra, and even of the Treasury, but taken at midday, the colors molten gold and bright blue, and taken from a slightly different angle from his.

They'd both been fascinated by Petra as students and had talked of visiting one day. Well, they both had. That they both had a photo of Petra as a cellphone screensaver showed that the city in ruins meant as much to her as it did to him.

This was Anya's cellphone. His cell was nowhere to be seen.

And she didn't have any security at all. No fingerprint, no password. Just her unsecured phone. He was going to bawl her out just as soon as this was over. She couldn't have an unsecured phone. But he tucked that away in the back of his mind. Right now, he needed to contact Joe Farris, his best friend and head of security.

He punched in Farris's cell and listened to the ringing. One, two, three ... then it went to voicemail. What the fuck? That was Farris's work number and he always answered.

Cal punched the number in again, impatiently listening to the rings then the switch to voicemail. "Yo, you know who this is and you know what to do."

Frustrated, he punched the numbers in with violence, as if that would make Farris pick up faster.

Waiting for the connection and the rings, he saw something on the floor and bent to pick it up, ignoring his swimming head.

A scrap of very pretty black lace. Oh God. Anya's panties. A pang of fear shot through him so strong it almost brought him to his knees. She was gone. Someone *had* her, maybe someone was hurting her *right this minute.*

Listening to the rings, Cal stuffed the small piece of Anya he had in his hand into his tux jacket pocket. His hand encountered something small and hard and he pulled it out just as he heard the voicemail message again.

Well, fuck. His head wasn't working right.

Farris had been working as hard as Cal had. Today was his first day off in four months and he said he was going out on a date with a pretty aid worker he'd met in Jordan. He was going to check out a five star restaurant he'd heard about in Chioggia, about forty clicks from Venice.

Farris wasn't answering not because he didn't want to — day off or no day off, Farris would always answer Cal's calls — but because he didn't recognize the number.

What was wrong with him?

He punched out a text. *Answer your fucking phone. C*

He studied what he had in his hand and which had definitely not been in his tux jacket pocket when he'd put the jacket on. It was small, black, featureless. Suddenly, with a rush of recognition, he realized what it was. A tracker. A fucking tracking device.

And he knew exactly who'd put it in his pocket. The fucking CIA in the person of Ash Fucking Morris.

Who was a dead man walking.

Anya's phone rang. The Stones' *You can't always get what you want.*

"Cal," Farris's deep voice came on. "'Sup? Whose phone are you on?"

"Mystery woman's." Cal had once gotten very very drunk with Farris as one more affair ended in tears and recriminations on the part of the woman, and all because the woman hadn't been Anya. He'd told Farris a little bit about the love of his life without naming names. Ever since then Farris talked about Mystery Woman.

There was no exclamation of startled surprise. Farris had been a Navy SEAL and had had the surprise beaten out of him a long time ago. As usual, Farris went right to the heart of the matter.

"So, are you in trouble?" Because why else would Cal be calling, from the phone of the one who got away?

"Yeah. I reconnected with her, a woman named Anya Voronova."

"Jesus. Deputy Director of Peace and Jobs?"

"Fuck. How do you know that?"

"It's my job to keep track of all the players, boss. Your job is to provide people with water so they can live."

Cal clenched his fist with the little tracker. It bit into the palm of his hand. He wanted to crush it like he wanted to crush the head of Ash Morris.

"They took her," he said simply. The words hurt his throat, as if knives were cutting him from inside out. "I think that fucker Ash Morris is behind it."

"Dr. Voronova? She's been kidnapped?"

Cal nodded, then realized Farris couldn't see him. He hadn't activated the video function. "Yeah," he said hoarsely.

"Are you at the reception at Palazzo Maltese?"

God. Cal pressed the heels of his hands against his eyes. He'd been knocked out, but he was also freaking at the idea of Anya in kidnappers' hands. He wasn't thinking straight, hadn't even reported where he was. Thank God Farris was thinking straight.

"Yeah. We were in a private room on the mezzanine when four or five men broke in. I took two of them down but I was sprayed with a knockout gas. Chloroform, I think. That was —" He checked his watch. "I was out for over a quarter of an hour. She could be anywhere by now."

"Does she have your phone?"

Cal looked around. His phone was gone. "She must. We both —" he swallowed heavily. "We both have the same model phone and the same case."

"With the Klingon word for peace?"

"Yeah. So she probably grabbed my phone."

"Then you know how to find her," Farris said simply.

Cal blanked. His brain simply turned off, overloaded with stress and fear for Anya. He clutched Anya's cell with one hand and the tracker with the other. Some strangled sound must have escaped his throat.

"Our app. The SecureFind app," Farris said patiently.

"Oh fuck," Cal breathed. "I forgot all about it."

His entire team in the field had an app that allowed everyone to know everyone else's whereabouts. They worked in rough and dangerous places and the app was always on in the field. They all turned it off when they went out to play.

"Is yours on?"

Cal thought frantically. Was his on? Had he turned it off? No, he'd forgotten to turn it off. "Yeah. But I don't have the program on this phone."

He could hear the sounds of an engine revving. "I'm sending you the app. Load it onto that phone and I'm sending you your code, because it sounds like fear has turned you stupid."

Cal had no answer to that.

"Don't worry, big guy. We'll get her back. I should be in the center of town in about forty to fifty minutes. Coming as fast as I can."

A beep, the incoming program. Cal feverishly loaded it,

loaded his personal code and dear sweet God, there it was! A blue teardrop shape laid over the map of Venice. Venice was anything but a grid, small winding streets haphazardly interspaced with bridges. Dense and confusing, a bewildering maze.

She was in a small street behind St. Mark's Square, a calle. Calle Venusio. The teardrop was moving. They wouldn't hurt her on the streets would they? Surely as long as they were moving, she was safe.

God only knew.

Cal made for the door at a run.

7

A nya stumbled repeatedly and would have fallen several times if not for the hard arm holding her up.

It was fake. She had excellent balance, but she wanted to delay the moment when they arrived wherever it was they were going.

Presumably the men would have taken off their balaclavas out on the streets. True, it was Mardi Gras — *Carnevale* — but people wore fancy costumes, not black fatigues with ski masks. Were they wearing other types of masks? She couldn't see them but she was starting to sort them out.

Outside the Palazzo, they'd been joined by the man who'd walked into the room in Palazzo Maltese. The American with an eastern seaboard upper class drawl. The man who'd been dressed in costume as a musketeer. Though she couldn't see him, she recognized the voice.

The three soldiers were Chinese who spoke decent English with the American. Between themselves they spoke Chinese — standard Mandarin, with no regional accents.

The American was coordinating something on his cell, speaking quietly. She could barely hear his words, catching one word in ten. Something about a journalist and the signing of the Accords tomorrow.

They appeared to be walking along side streets, narrow ones, so narrow that sounds echoed off the walls. The further they got from St. Mark's Square, the fewer people there were.

For a while she was escorted by two men, one on each side, but at a corner, one fell away. The one who remained kept the gun pressed to her right side. She put out her left hand and felt a wall. A calle so narrow more than two people had difficulty walking side by side.

They were close to the action, though. The sounds of thousands and thousands of revelers was close by, footsteps clanging on the cobblestones and voices raised in merriment. It was so hard not to call out for help. But a gun pressed to her rib cage was a great deterrent.

Her hand dropped to her side and she tore another black bead off the skirt and surreptitiously let it drop close to the wall where she hoped it wouldn't be kicked away. She'd been pulling beads off and dropping them all along the way, like the breadcrumbs dropped by Hansel and Gretel. Hoping it would lead Cal to her.

Another bead.

Such a flimsy hope. Hopes. Hope that he'd wake up soon from the chloroform. That no one had stayed behind to hurt him so badly he couldn't get up or — she shuddered at the thought — to shoot him with a suppressed gun. The gun stuck in her side had an extra long slim barrel — it was suppressed.

If they shot her, no one would hear.

And now they were headed into very narrow side streets that were deserted. The Mardi Gras revelers wanted to see and be seen. The streets they were walking on were all but empty.

Anya was very aware that her life hung by a thread, a series of improbable things having to happen if she were to be rescued. It all depended on Cal. On his coming to consciousness soon. On his being able to take action. On him finding the beads and following the breadcrumbs to where she was. On being able to deal with an armed man, or armed men, if and when the miracle occurred and he was able to find her.

So very unlikely.

But then this was *Cal*, who'd always confounded expectations and always *always* did better than anyone could hope. He'd come from a terrible family background — mother gone, alcoholic father. But he'd always been so very smart and so very strong and had triumphed, always.

And ... he loved her.

Loved her still.

If he *could* come, he would.

She just had to stay alive long enough.

A hard hand jerked her to a halt and she purposefully stumbled into the man in front of her. He cursed in Chinese, using a couple of words she'd never heard before as the gunman's hand tightened painfully.

"I'll leave you to it," the American said. "I'll coordinate as soon as you get the intel."

"Shi."

"Shi."

Yes.

Oh God. Two brand new men answered. There were now

four men, she thought, at least one of them armed. She swayed for a moment and it wasn't fake.

She tore off and dropped two beads.

It was oddly quiet here. They must have been in a cul de sac because the sounds of Mardi Gras revelry were faint and far away, barely audible. She heard hinges squeaking, a door opening. She was turned and pushed hard. The inside of the building was chillier than outside, a blast of musty frigid air forming almost a barrier between the outside world and the inside of the building.

Anya was dragged over the threshold and this time her stumbles were real. The man holding her cursed, his fingers digging into the flesh of her arm to keep her upright.

She was marched across a large empty space, noise echoing in the void, to a door across the room. The inside of that room seemed large and empty too. She was marched across it and into another room until she banged her shin painfully against something wooden. A chair. Anya reached out and touched it. Large, solid, more a throne than a chair.

The man who held her arm pushed her unexpectedly and she collapsed into the large chair. A ripping sound and she could feel her ankles being taped together. So — this was going to be an interrogation and not a rape.

The area at the edge of her mask lit up. There was a bright light in the room.

"Take off your mask," one of the men said.

She reached behind her head to untie the satin ribbons, immediately raising her hand against the light as the mask fell. Some kind of spotlight was shining in her face, so bright it hurt. It was impossible to make out any faces behind the light, which was the purpose, she imagined.

"There must be some mistake," she said, glad that her

voice was cool. Twice she'd been in a room facilitating negotiations where violence was threatened. She knew how to mask her feelings.

"No mistake," a deep male baritone answered. "You're here for a reason." She tried hard to analyze the voice. Educated, cultivated. Detached, even faintly amused. Slight foreign accent.

She'd never heard that voice before.

"Do you know who I am?"

"Of course," the voice answered. "Anya Voronova. Deputy Director of Peace and Jobs."

Yes. They wanted *her*, Anya Voronova. But for what? Anya's job was not highly classified. She hadn't been privy to the top levels of negotiation. Peace and Jobs dealt with humdrum matters like educational curricula, equal pay for equal work, access to health care, job safety. It was possible that people at levels much higher than hers had secrets that someone could want, but she definitely didn't.

She used the only weapon she had at her disposal, one that had worked before, though not always. Reason.

"If you're looking for a ransom, you're out of luck. Peace and Jobs operates on a shoestring. And we're going to downsize considerably after the Accords are signed. Trust me when I tell you that no one has any money to pay for me."

A sigh. "Oh, we're not after money, Dr. Voronova."

Anya's blood chilled. He'd done his research, used her academic title. Anya never used her title in the field. She could too easily be mistaken for a medical doctor.

These men, whoever they were, were not after money. To her surprise, money was the most innocent of all the barriers to peace she'd encountered. Money was easy. But eliminate money and you had hatred and resentment and vengeance.

It had to be asked. "What are you after, then?"

He sighed and stepped forward. Not enough that she could see his face, but enough that she could make out his form. He was holding some kind of long stick. Was he going to beat her with it? You could break bones with sticks, she knew. Break bones, break skin, concuss. A lot of bad things could be done with a stick.

Then he reached out to her and touched her arm with one end and it wasn't a stick. It was an electric prod.

Pain. Pain. Pain.

Pain that filled the world, filled her whole body, from head to toe.

Shocked, she arched back in the chair, head back, and screamed with the pain. Her entire body was on fire, nerve endings aflame, the pain crackling, alive. She drew her breath in to scream again and ...

It stopped. Suddenly. She slumped back into her seat. The only sign anything had happened was her heart beating triple time, trying to beat its way out of her chest.

She looked down at herself, at her arms, hands. They were perfectly normal. Instinctively, she checked her skin, expecting it to be blackened and blistered. But no, she was unblemished. All she had to show for the period of excruciating pain was a little soreness in her muscles.

The man spoke in a calm, unhurried tone. "That was just a little teaser, Dr Voronova. The shock lasted twenty seconds though I have no doubt that for you it was a very long twenty seconds. I also have no doubt that the pain was severe. This is a new...device. Weapon, really. Designed for close combat and extreme crowd control. It has a little dial on the side. The setting right now is the lowest possible. So what you just felt is the very best of what you're going to feel. Did I make myself clear?"

He was going to torture her and there would be no marks whatsoever. She nodded.

"Was I clear, Dr Voronova?" he repeated, voice a little sharper.

"Yes." Her voice was weak, strained. Showing this much strain at the first show of what he could do put her in a very weak position. She cleared her throat, made her voice as strong as she could. "Yes, that was very clear."

She could make out his head, bowing. "Excellent. You have spirit. But then I would expect nothing less of the deputy director of Peace and Jobs. So." He clapped his hands together. "We're off to an excellent start."

Oh God. Anya tried to gather as much information as she could. The more she understood her situation, the better she could resist. But there was almost nothing to understand.

She'd completely lost track while being walked through the streets of Venice essentially blinded. She knew Venice well but it was more a maze than anything else. Even Venetians could get lost if they didn't have visual markers. They'd walked along St. Mark's Square for about three minutes and she'd heard revelers but then they'd turned a corner and entered the labyrinth of Venice's small backstreets.

She hadn't stood a chance.

The people she'd heard in their trek to where they were now had been Italians, but also Germans, Swedes and a few French. Venice's population doubled during *Carnevale*, and there were also the people who'd come to celebrate the signing of the Accords.

Everyone was in a happy, celebratory mood. Even if she'd

managed to break away or catch their attention, surely they'd have taken it as a joke.

She remembered a saying a Venetian friend had taught her. *A Carnevale ogni scherzo vale.* Anything goes during Mardi Gras.

She was sure they were in the maze of small back alleys close to the Grand Canal. The brackish smell of sea water had permeated the air but most of Venice smelled of the sea. She listened hard for the sound of waves lapping to know if they fronted one of the side canals but it was quiet. The moldy ancient walls were made of stone. No sounds penetrated. And her screams wouldn't be heard.

They'd chosen this place well.

Besides her tormentor, she could count two men behind the blinding light — shadowy figures. No chance of identifying them, which is what the light was about. Plus the two voices who were probably standing guard. Not many men, just five of them. Cal could probably dispatch them easily, if they didn't gas him. He'd taken care of two back at Palazzo Maltese before being put under.

Well, she sure wasn't going to fight her way out of this. Though she'd taken self defense classes because her work took her to dangerous places, there was no way she could overwhelm five men. And certainly not hobbled as she was.

Plus at least one man was armed. There was a good chance all of them were now, if this was their headquarters.

So that was her situation. She didn't know where she was and she didn't know who her kidnappers were and she didn't know what they wanted from her.

"So, Dr Voronova, bearing in mind that I can increase the voltage to ten times what I administered, when was the last time you spoke with your friend June Chen."

What? Anya blanked. "June Chen? I don't remember —"
Searing pain.

Unbelievable hot, spiky, rending pain that went on and on, like someone dragging barbed wire over her skin.

When it stopped, tears were streaming down her face. Her throat felt raw. She must have screamed though she had no memory of it. She had no memory of anything but the pain.

"Wrong answer," the man answered mildly. Then — "Let's try this once again. When was the last time you heard from your friend June Chen?"

Anya's mind was sluggish. She could barely remember five minutes ago let alone a period in the past. The man pushed the rod toward her and she shouted, "Stop!"

It stopped, half a foot from her arm. It waited there, like something alive. Like a snake ready to strike.

Anya rubbed her forehead. "June Chen? Wait. We had lunch in Istanbul. A couple of months ago, end of November. She'd just won a big journalism prize for her article on the Bedouin."

She and June had been friends for a long time, ever since June had interviewed her early in the negotiations for the Accords and tried to get Anya to bad-mouth the Chinese government. At the time, the official line of the Central Committee had been hostility to the Accords. A month later, a new President had been overwhelmingly voted into power, Hu Lin. Hu was a modernizer and very much in favor of the Accords. But back then, the government line was that the Accords were a Western conspiracy to sabotage Chinese economic growth.

June had tried to get Anya to criticize the Chinese government.

It would have been easy to give out strong signals of exasperation, because Anya had been working hard to get the Chinese to cooperate, but Anya was an old diplomatic hand and had given June nothing. Then she'd signaled June to turn off her cell recorder and to go off the record. After which, she'd told June that the Chinese government sucked rocks.

They'd both laughed and had had a boozy lunch and bonded over the terrible quality of the single men working on the Accord. They all sucked rocks, too.

Anya's statement had stayed off the record but she and June had been really good friends since then.

So," the man said, the rod still unwaveringly half a foot from her arm. She watched it with horror. "You last saw June in Istanbul? In November?"

"Yes." Anya nodded.

"Wrong answer," he said and jabbed her with the prod.

Pain. Pain. Pain.

Intense, unceasing agony, prolonged this time. Though it was hard to tell because the pain was something out of time. Time stopped as the world became agony, burning, suffering.

When the rod pulled away from her skin, Anya was sweating, tears running down her face. She looked down at her skin, again sure she'd see blood and blisters, but all she saw was smooth skin. It had felt like being flayed alive, inch by inch.

In a church in Venice she'd seen a famous painting by Tiepolo, *The Flaying of St Bartholomew* and had nearly been reduced to tears at the sight of the knife slicing into the martyr's skin, the skin pulled up and away from the living flesh.

It had felt just like that.

The other shadowy figures were exactly where they'd been before, completely unmoved by her torment.

"As the movie line goes, Dr Voronova, I can do this all day. And all night and all the next day. And if I grow tired, my colleagues here —" he moved slowly to the left and the right, "can continue while I go out for a nice restaurant meal and a rest. So you might as well give me what I need."

What she needed was all her wits about her. These people wanted something from her but she didn't know what. Her mind was sluggish, like walking through mud.

Her head hung low, as if the strings holding her head up had been cut. "I'd like to give you what you need, but —"

He zapped her again.

Agony.

There was no getting used to it, no bracing herself, no way to psychologically prepare for the torment. It was as horrible as the first time, even more so. She blanked with the pain, nothing in her worked, she shook and hurt and endured.

The pain stopped.

Anya looked down at her trembling hands, surprised all over again that no blood was showing.

A heavy sigh from the man. The rod was still half a foot from her. She hadn't seen it come toward her and she hadn't seen it retracted. It was just this monstrous, mysterious thing that came out of nowhere and hovered. Able to dispense crippling agony at any moment.

"So, again, just for your information, that was the low setting, Doctor. I can ratchet it up, though it might rattle your thinking afterward. I need you to be lucid. I need you to remember."

Was there a timeline? Anya wondered. Was he in a hurry? Was that why he was shocking her so often? Was it just a question of waiting him out? And how on earth could she do that when every touch of that prod was searing agony? Surely her heart would give out?

"June Chen, Dr. Voronova. You talked to her today."

Anya shook her head. Not in negation but in confusion. "What? I didn't talk to June today. I told you, I haven't seen her since —"

Pain.

It must have been longer or stronger, or something. Anya came to after a million years, exhausted and confused.

And terrified.

Was she going to die here, in this cold room smelling of mold and rot? Alone and scared? Watched by these monstrous men?

"Around noon, Doctor," the man continued as if they were having an unhurried conversation interrupted by a waiter bringing drinks. "You spoke with June Chen around noon."

Anya rolled that around in her head, the words a jumble that made no sense. June ... at noon. It even rhymed.

She closed her eyes and this time felt a sharp pain on her arm, not electric. He'd whapped her with the rod instead of zapping her.

"Are we boring you, Dr Voronova?" he asked, voice dripping acid.

She sat straighter in the uncomfortable chair, trying to sharpen her wits. But she was exhausted and afraid.

"N-no." She waited. He waited. "Not bored."

"Excellent. So let's take it again from the top. You spoke

with June Chen around noon today. I want to know what Ms. Chen said to you."

Anya's mind raced. She was trying to be brave but the fear of the prod, of that excruciating pain, overrode everything. Was he right? Could she have spoken with June without remembering? Without knowing about it? How could that be? At noon she was — a wave of relief washed through her. Maybe this was a horrible mistake and she could just correct him and they'd let her go. She'd find Cal and they'd —

"*Dr. Voronova!*" The man's voice was loud and sharp. She jumped.

"S-sorry. I couldn't have spoken with June. I was in a meeting all day, the Cross Frontier Jobs Committee, until around 5 p.m. I barely made it back to my hotel in time to dress for the reception."

Zap!

Anya was trembling all over now, hands and legs. This time there was a lingering pain, as if her nerves had soaked up the electricity and were releasing it even after the prod was removed.

"The conversation between the two of you was overheard. You're lying."

Her throat was so dry she couldn't speak. Lips dry, tongue so dry it stuck to the roof of her mouth. "Water," she croaked. "Please."

A huge sigh of exasperation. The outline of the man gestured with his head. The light was angled to shine directly into her eyes and it was turned up. A hand held out a bottle of water but she couldn't make out any features. Not the face, not the shape of the body.

She grabbed the bottle with shaking hands. It took her

three attempts to crack the bottle cap and she spilled half the contents raising the small bottle to her mouth. The water felt wonderful going down her throat but she stopped after a few gulps.

Those shocks were going to continue because she couldn't give him what he wanted. Didn't have it to give. If her stomach was full of water she could vomit it back up, choke on it while being zapped.

But at least she could talk now. "I haven't seen June since Istanbul. I swear. You can zap me forever and that won't change. I haven't seen her today, didn't see her yesterday. The last time I saw her was over lunch three months ago. And I was in a meeting all day today. There are records of my presence during the meeting. You can check the minutes. I was there, in the meeting room, from ten to five. We didn't even break for lunch, they brought in sandwiches. You can check. Please check."

Silence.

Her voice had been shaky but it rang with sincerity. She hadn't seen June today, she hadn't seen anyone during the day except for the committee members. She hoped these men believed her because she had nothing else to offer but the truth.

Behind the blinding light she could see shadowy heads conferring. They were whispering and she couldn't grasp anything of what they were saying.

The man spoke again. "She called you, Dr. Voronova. Called you and left a message."

Anya opened her mouth and then closed it. For the first time, she realized she could be putting June in danger. It was possible that June had called her on her personal cell while she was in a meeting. She'd checked her work cell and there had been no messages.

If June had left her a message, would these men go after *her* then? It was so hard to think straight but her head wasn't necessary. Her heart told her all she needed to know. June was a dear friend and a smart, fearless journalist on top of that. Anya was not going to do anything that could put June in peril.

A long arm reached out for her purse and her spirits sank. Her personal cell was in there. If June had left a text or a message, they would read it or listen to it.

Her interrogator unsnapped her purse and pulled out her cell, holding it so she could see *Roj*. Anya's chest tightened with fear for June. He swiped the screen, then held it out to her, screen facing her. "Password," he ordered.

Her thinking was so *slow*. Thoughts jumbled and muddled. Her first thought was — *I don't have a password.* Her work cell had a password, of course. Peace and Jobs was transparent and didn't have many secrets, but sometimes the people they negotiated with didn't want their willingness to work for peace known. So their phones were password protected and their computers encrypted. Nothing military-grade, but also not that easy to crack.

But her work phone was back in the hotel room. Peace and Jobs had basically fulfilled its mandate. As a matter of fact, Anya was preparing to look for a new job. They'd done the impossible and it was time to move on. The Accords were to be signed tomorrow and the reception tonight was a purely social affair. She hadn't wanted her work phone. The secretariat of the Accords had her personal cell number for the family photo because Anya had given it to them.

The man held out the cell, screen lit up, and there was

her screensaver. A snapshot she'd taken with her phone of the Treasury at Petra. She and Cal both had been fascinated by Petra and when she finally made it there, she'd almost cried because she wasn't with Cal.

But wait — it *wasn't* her screensaver. It was a photo of Petra, true, but instead of at high noon, the buildings intense molten gold, it was a shot taken at dawn, the colors a tenuous light blue and pale gold. And the angle was wrong.

This — this wasn't her cell, it was Cal's. And not only did they have the exact same case, they both had almost the exact same screensaver.

Proof once again of the intense bond they shared, even after ten years.

But there was a keypad superimposed on the photo of Petra, and it required a password.

Since this was Cal's phone, there was no way in the world she could know the password. There was just no way she could access this phone.

Even if she could convince this man that it wasn't her phone, that her phone — with presumably a message from June — was in Cal's hands, that meant they'd go after Cal.

Anya's spine stacked as she sat straighter, though all her muscles were trembling.

No.

She would not give Cal up. She would not give June up. She'd rather die.

8

C al was trembling. From the aftereffects of the chloroform he'd been dosed with, from the blow to the head and from absolute fucking terror. Fear like he'd never known before made him shake and sweat.

Anya was in the hands of terrorists. They had to be terrorists. Who else could they be? There had always been violent factions in the Middle East opposed to peace, as against the overwhelming majority of people who just wanted to lead normal lives, raise families, look to the future with hope.

A lot of people said that terrorism was dead but Cal knew better. The terrorists weren't dead, they'd just been driven underground like rats.

And now Anya ... Christ, he couldn't even go there.

He'd seen videos that no human should ever have to see.

He feverishly followed a teardrop shape on his screen that represented the love of his life. The only woman he'd ever loved. The only woman he ever would love. He knew that now.

In the hallway outside the room where they'd reunited, there were three black beads. His love — his smart, smart love — had done what she could to leave breadcrumbs for him to follow. He rushed down the wide hallway where another broad hallway intersected. Left or right? He wasn't familiar with Palazzo Maltese. He knew where Anya was at the moment but he needed to take the fastest route there.

Scanning the hallways to the left and to the right he saw two small jet beads on the right hand side and immediately turned right. At the end of that long hallway was a set of elaborately carved French windows that gave out on a stone terrace. In the four corners of the terrace four torches flickered. Cal scoured the terrace and saw a small jet bead right where a set of stone steps led down into a tiny garden.

The screen showed the teardrop slowing down.

He studied the screen which was a map of the historic center of the city of Venice. It was a city map designed to reduce an engineer to tears. Not one straight line. A series of curving narrow streets, some looping back on themselves, most with bridges crossing a canal every twenty meters or so.

But Cal could follow. He liked order as much as the next engineer but he'd worked in Middle Eastern cities for the past five years and he was used to the tight whorls of the labyrinths that were ancient cities. The orientation lobe in his head — which was very strong — straightened out the path he had to take.

He was still woozy and in pain but that made no difference at all to him. He'd get to Anya if he had to walk through hell itself, barefoot over broken glass. A little pain was nothing.

The teardrop stopped. Wherever they were taking Anya, they were there.

His eyes tracked back and forth across the narrow streets. He wasn't looking for beads. It didn't make any difference now what path she'd taken. He knew where she was now. What he needed was a weapon. Wherever Anya had been taken, she was now a prisoner.

In the field, Cal was always armed, even if he had a phalanx of his security team with him at all times. He was good with arms, too. He had excellent reflexes and eye-hand coordination and he made sure he kept his marksmanship alive and active.

But Cal didn't trust guns. He trusted himself, his body. He was decent with arms but he was really good in unarmed close-quarter combat. Still, right now he'd have given his right arm for a gun. He was going to need it, or need ... something.

Whoever had come for Anya — and he'd lay odds they were somehow tied to that fucker Ash — had been able to overpower him. He'd been taken by surprise, it was true. That wouldn't happen again. But the truth was, no matter how good he was at martial arts, if there were four or five men wherever Anya had been taken, he was fucked. Particularly if they were armed.

So he needed a weapon.

He called Farris, the sound of a car engine loud in the background. Farris liked sports cars and he'd be speeding. "Yo, man. Coming."

"Yeah, I know. Are you armed?"

Short silence. "Who are you talking to?"

"Former Navy SEAL."

"Then you've got your answer. Now let me drive." Farris disconnected.

So Farris would bring a weapon. Several, if he knew his guy, and he did. But Farris was on his way and not here yet. No matter what, Cal wasn't waiting for him. He was getting there now.

The teardrop had stopped at a building. Cal enlarged the screen. Phoenix was an engineering company, one of the finest in the world. The map was excellent. The more he zoomed in, the finer the detail until he was looking at a 3D map of an area off the beaten path on the other side of the island.

It had taken them almost half an hour to get there, dragging an unwilling hostage. Even under threat, Anya would have slowed them down as much as she dared. Cal could get there in ten minutes.

Several of the streets he walked along were thronged with *Carnevale* revelers. He heard ten languages in so many minutes.

He heard a trill of female laughter and three beautiful women made up as 17th-century courtesans were walking along one of the alleys, arm in arm. They completely closed off the narrow street.

Guarda che bello! One of them exclaimed. Cal knew enough Italian to recognize the compliment. What a handsome guy!

They were going to slow him down if he didn't play this right. It was against his nature to push women out of his way but they looked a little drunk and ready to rumble and he couldn't afford the time.

Moving fast, he gently lifted the arms of two of the beautiful women, stooped and slipped between them murmuring, *signore scusate*, and continued. He was at the end of the street, climbing a steeply arched bridge before they realized what happened. A couple of seconds later, he turned to the right, paralleling the canal, and their exclamations were swallowed up.

This part of the city was almost deserted. It was a strange thing about Venice. Some streets were so crowded you couldn't breathe, but turn a corner or two and you were completely alone.

He was running now, the sounds of his footfalls echoing off the stone walls. He cursed everything about his situation, including the goddamned brand-new dress shoes that slipped on the cobblestones. He longed for his desert boots. The tux bow tie felt like it was about to strangle him. He hooked a finger underneath it, pulled it off and threw it away.

The teardrop was three short streets and a bridge away. He desperately needed something ... ah! He was running by a restoration site. Part of a wall had crumbled and it was being restored manually. The workers had tucked tools away in a box inside the wall. Cal bent and picked up a chisel. Strong wooden handle, sharp edges. Good for tearing someone's throat out. He picked up a big heavy mallet, too, and slipped both into his cummerbund. Finally a cummerbund that was useful for something.

But he needed something else, something with more reach.

Though his head was drumming *hurry hurry hurry,* he took his time. Bringing a knife to a gun fight was never a good idea, so it better be a good knife. He found what he needed in a pile of rubble. A construction rod. He picked it up, hefted it. Strong and straight and about a yard in length.

He would relish pounding in the head of anyone who'd hurt Anya.

Ok. The teardrop was still. The GPS system said where Anya was horizontally, but didn't tell him where Anya was vertically. He knew the building she was in but not exactly where in that building she was. And that was assuming she was near his phone. If it had been dropped or thrown away, he was in a shitload of trouble because the beads had stopped a couple of streets back.

The faintest vibration from Anya's cell. A text message from Farris.

20 mikes out

He was twenty minutes out. But Cal had already arrived.

The entrance to the building was on Calle Aosta, right around the corner. He crouched and held the cell out past the corner wall, in video mode, positioning the screen so he had a good view of the entrance of the building.

And ... fuck. A sentry. A fucking *armed* sentry. The man was dressed in black, unnaturally thick around the torso with body armor and had a shoulder holster, with a pistol in his hand. They must be very sure of themselves to walk around armed in Venice. Probably they had worn jackets while walking the crowded streets.

Or maybe the drunken revelers just assumed they were in costume. Modern-day ninja warriors. Not the usual *Carnevale* costumes, but then he'd been told that the usual fancy 17th-century costumes were being replaced by cosplay costumes, with lots of Batmen and Wonder Women.

Well, though dressed in a traditional tux, Cal had a hammer and he was now fucking *Thor*.

He studied the geometry of the situation. The walls, the position of the sentry, the distance to the doorway. He could do this.

He waited until the sentry was in the exact right position, back to him, looking north. Cal rose from his crouch, mallet in hand and threw it overhand as hard as he could right at the back of the fucker's head.

It seemed to float in slow motion, handle over hammerhead, calculated perfectly to smash into the back of the sentry's head at top speed.

The sentry dropped like a stone without a sound.

Good.

Cal rushed over to him, retrieved the mallet, picked up the guy's pistol, checked the magazine, checked that there was a round in the chamber and kicked the sentry out of the way without a second glance.

From inside the building came a woman's scream of pain.

Anya.

Someone was hurting Anya.

He slid into the doorway silent as a ghost. He felt like a ninja — invincible and invisible. And even if they saw him, it didn't make any difference because they were going *down*.

The building was empty. Some kind of warehouse that was rarely used. Empty crates were stacked up against a wall and the stench of mold was overwhelming. He slid against the walls, a black shadow in darkness. Another man stood guard against an internal doorway. The room beyond was dark but a bright light came from the room beyond that one. He heard a man's voice talking, a low woman's voice answering.

Then her scream of pain.

Cal stopped for a moment and breathed down his rage. A man, hurting Anya. He was going to pay, oh God was he going to pay. But Cal had to make his way to the back room slowly because the man tormenting her was close to Anya, could hurt her badly.

No guns. It reinforced his bias against weaponry. In this building, even a silenced weapon would be heard. No. This had to be done the old fashioned way.

Cal slid around the walls until he was to the side of the sentry but not close enough to touch. Any closer and he'd be sensed. An ancient Druse in Beirut who'd been at war all his life had once explained that humans have an unnamed sense that allows them to feel the presence of other humans before they can see them.

Cal waited until the sentry looked toward the distant room. The light from the room would impair his night vision. When the man turned his back, Cal struck.

His movements were smooth and fast. He slid the iron bar from his cummerbund and slammed it into the back of the man's head. The only sounds were the slight whoosh of the iron bar through the air and the slight squelch as it struck the man. Nothing that could be heard from even a foot away.

The man was on the floor, a pool of blood slowly staining the floor beneath his head. Cal slid the iron rod back under his cummerbund, grabbed the man's feet and dragged him further from the doorway so he couldn't be seen from inside the room where Anya was.

He slid around the door, being very quiet but he needn't have bothered. No one was paying attention to anything. They were paying attention to Anya.

Oh god, there she was. Trapped in a chair, feet taped

together. She was paper white, face drawn, tear tracks still wet on her cheeks.

A spotlight had been brought in, beaming right in her eyes. She was effectively blinded.

"You will tell us the password to your phone, Dr Voronova. You will break eventually." There he was. Anya's torturer, holding what looked like a high-tech rod.

Anya lifted her head, those light blue eyes dimmed. There was no defiance in her voice or in her body language. This was a broken woman. But still, she answered. "No."

To Cal's horror, the man lifted his arm and reached out to touch Anya with the end of that long steel rod. Cal had just bashed in the head of someone with a rod. No one was going to do that to Anya. His muscles bunched to leap forward when he noticed that the man wasn't bringing his arm back for a blow. On the contrary, he was reaching out slowly, giving her time to react.

It wouldn't be a killing blow.

Thank God Cal had hesitated because he saw now what he hadn't noticed before, all his attention focused on Anya.

There were two other men in the room. Very fit men with guns. Both men were carrying QSZ-92 pistols, which were standard issue in the Chinese police force. They carried a Parabellum round that would shred Anya to pieces. The rounds left the barrel at a minimum velocity of 230 meters per second. The pistol was not accurate beyond fifty meters but it didn't have to be. Both men were only a few meters away from Anya. And him.

Cal had to factor himself in. He'd gladly sacrifice himself to save Anya but the chances were good that he'd get one guy before being gunned down by the other and then Anya would be at the mercy of two angry men with automatic weapons.

He had to study this carefully.

All of that nearly went out the window when Anya's tormentor touched Anya with his rod and she stiffened, head arched, eyes rolled back in her head, shaking all over. Though her lips were pressed together, a moan escaped her that escalated into a scream.

The fucker was tasing her! No, not tasing. There were no spikes with wires. Some kind of ... of *cattle prod* designed for humans. Used on Anya!

Cal clutched the door jamb to keep from flinging himself into the room. But risky as it was, he couldn't stand here and let Anya be tortured, simply couldn't.

He tapped the construction rod twice on the stone floor and pulled behind the wall just in time as the man with the prod turned.

A command in what sounded like Chinese and then the sound of boot heels. Fuckers were so sure of themselves they didn't even attempt stealth. They had a helpless woman at their mercy. They felt like big men.

One of the guards walked across the threshold into the dark room where Cal waited.

Take this! Cal thought viciously, as he slammed the callused and hardened edge of his hand into the man's throat with all the fury in his body. The man went down without a sound. He was incapable of sound because Cal has smashed his voicebox together with his windpipe. Cal eased him to the ground silently.

Three down, two to go.

The tormentor issued a sharp command. Probably

calling his guards. Not panicked but aware there was an enemy in the house.

You have no idea, Cal thought.

From inside the room he heard an electronic beep then a voice. "Send backup. We have an intruder." He'd called for help.

Cal didn't care. He could have called for the fucking Chinese Army, these guys were going down.

Anya screamed.

"Come out!" the guy called. "Come out or I'll bring a world of hurt down on her." Anya moaned, breathing heavily as the guy pulled away the rod from her arm.

Cal was good at spatial orientation. He knew where everyone in the room was. He was an engineer, but it was also a gift he'd always had. It made him good at sports and it made him an excellent martial artist.

And he had a killer aim.

"Come —" the man began but Cal's mallet was already making his way to the fucker's head. Before it hit, he sprang into action, leading with the chisel, punching into the second fuckhead's chest and then pivoting and slamming his foot into his knee, shattering it. The man went down with a scream, dropping his weapon.

Cal kicked away the gun and ran to Anya. Her eyes widened. "Cal!" She pointed a shaking hand to the ground.

The guy whose knee he'd shattered was pulling a knife from a sheath. Well ... good. Cal needed that knife. He stepped on the guy's hand hard enough to hear the wrist bones break, bent to pick the knife up and moved in one smooth motion to slice the tape around Anya's ankles.

She pointed again at the fucker who just wouldn't stay

down and was scrambling for his gun with his one good hand.

"Use that," Anya said, pointing to the rod that had fallen from the other guy's hand.

"I like the way you think, darling." Cal picked it up and studied it for one second. Simple mechanism. One button. Didn't need an engineering degree to operate. He jammed the rod against the man's ribs, hard, and pressed the button.

The man's back arched, one good leg skittering on the floor, eyes wide open in pain, a deep moan coming from his throat.

Cal kept it going far beyond what was necessary to keep the man down.

These fuckers had tortured Anya with that. He didn't care whether they lived or died.

When the man passed out, Cal lifted the rod, slamming it into the stone wall until the wiring came away then threw it into a corner of the room and crouched in front of Anya, the men already forgotten.

He watched her face carefully, prying the phone she held — his phone — from her hand. She was so goddamned pale. "Can you walk, honey?" he asked, putting his hand gently on her knee.

Anya's mouth turned down. "I don't know. Only one way to find out." She braced herself on the arms of the chair and pushed. Tried to stand, shakily. She'd have fallen if Cal hadn't caught her. He plastered a bland expression on his face because if he showed the rage he felt inside he'd have scared her.

He caught her up in his arms, his wonderful princess. He'd lost about ten years off his life in this past half hour. He was never going to let her out of his sight, ever *ever* again.

She tried on a smile for him. "Let's blow this joint, Cal. Food's bad and the music's worse."

His heart clenched. She must have felt what was roiling around inside him, rage and worry. She was trying to make light of having been tortured because it might upset him.

And, um, yeah. It fucking did.

He kicked one of the monsters out of his way, didn't even look down. "You got it, baby," he said and they walked out of the ancient, abandoned building together.

9

By the time they crossed a second bridge, Anya felt stronger. She knew herself and knew her body. It had taken a lot of punishment, but deep down, at some cellular level, she knew she'd recover.

Yet even when she was sure she could stand on her feet, she hesitated just a moment longer. It felt so delicious to be carried by Cal. It had been years and years — ten of them in fact, all of them hard — since she'd been able to count on anyone's strength other than her own.

They'd been such a team when they were together. Cal had carried a heavy academic workload besides his teaching duties. He was strong and a hard worker, but sometimes he would come home exhausted. She'd cook a nice meal, buy a bottle of wine and over the course of the meal, some color would come back into his tired face.

When she was tired, he'd rub her feet for her.

They both had known, instinctively, when they really needed each other.

Someone had been cooking meals for him, but no one had rubbed her feet since Cal.

There was a far-off background noise of revelry and thousands of feet but the noise fell away as they turned into a deserted calle. Cal showed no signs of being tired from carrying her, but they were far from safe. "Put me down, Cal," she murmured, raising her head from his shoulder.

He stopped, those compelling, light brown eyes staring into hers. "You sure?"

He asked seriously and she took the question seriously, doing an internal scan, head to toe and back. "Yes," she said decisively. "I'm sure."

He didn't question her, simply put her gently on her feet, keeping a big hand on her upper arm. If Cal was holding her, she could keep upright forever.

"I think we should —" Cal interrupted himself, cocking a head. He'd always had superb hearing. She heard it a full second later. A man talking, a one-sided conversation, in Chinese.

He glanced at her and she nodded. The man was looking for them, reporting in that contact hadn't been made yet.

Cal didn't need a translation. He pushed her gently against the brick wall and crouched. He was intending to attack before they were found. But then there was the sound of another set of boots on the cobblestoned street. She and Cal couldn't know whether more were around the corner. And they were probably armed. Cal was good but all it would take was an armed third guy to come while Cal was battling another two and Cal would go down with a bullet to the head. No martial artist can combat a bullet, no matter how good he is.

But there he was, center mass low to the ground, big hands flexing, ready to try to take them down.

They were in a cobblestoned lane with a vaulted roof. Not a street but a passageway, one of thousands criss-crossing the city. She narrowed her eyes as she looked behind her.

This passageway happened to be one she knew. A year ago, in Venice for negotiations, she'd broken her favorite umbrella, one her father had given her a long time ago. It had been a difficult period, she'd been working fourteen-hour days trying to get hostile delegates to sit down at the negotiating table to iron out final details and seemingly the only thing they could agree on was hostility towards Peace and Jobs and hatred of her, personally.

And in the middle of negotiations that felt like swal-lowing shards of glass, her beloved umbrella that repro-duced the dome of the Florence cathedral broke.

She'd been devastated. One of the secretaries, who'd become a close friend, had taken her to the last umbrella repairman in Venice, maybe the world, in this very lane. To her delight, he'd repaired the umbrella.

And the door to the umbrella repair shop was recessed.

She grabbed Cal's hand. "Come with me."

Everything hurt when she moved but she took them as quickly as she could halfway down the lane and — yes! — there it was. She'd remembered correctly.

The voices were louder and they tucked themselves into the recessed entrance just in time. There were at least three men, speaking low. But the walls were like echo chambers and the voices carried.

They were Chinese and were hunting them.

"Look carefully in each side street," one of them said.

Light bounced off the walls of the alleyway as they used powerful flashlights. If they hadn't been in the recessed doorway they'd have been caught.

"Check her phone," another one said and Anya froze. *Her phone!*

Cal felt her jolt and turned to her frowning. *What's wrong?*

She held her hand up to her ear, thumb and pinkie finger out, in the universal gesture for phone, and shook her head. *I left it behind.*

As always, they understood each other perfectly. He pulled one phone with the *Roj* case on the back out of his right hand pocket. She frowned and pointed to herself. *That's mine.*

He nodded, pointed his thumb at her. *It's yours.*

He pried off the case, opened the phone with a tiny screwdriver he produced from somewhere, removed the battery. Stuck his thumb down in a universal gesture. *It's dead now.*

She looked at him with an interrogatory scowl. *They can't follow the phone?*

He shook his head. *Absolutely not.* Held up another phone, his. Stuck his thumb up. *This is my phone. They can't follow it.*

Oh God, how she'd missed this. This instant understanding of each other. She could kiss him.

And she did.

They were already almost hugging. She lifted up and placed her mouth on his in a fleeting kiss which she stopped immediately. It was like a placeholder kiss. More to come.

Cal held his phone with one hand, his other arm around her. He speed dialed with his thumb and immediately said,

"It's me. Got my phone back." The person at the other end must have been waiting for the call. "Sitrep," he said quietly, then listened. After a moment, he thumbed the call closed.

"Help is stuck in traffic, sorry."

Well she wouldn't know where to find help. But he did.

Without thinking, Anya turned in Cal's arm, closed her arms around his neck and kissed him again.

And kissed him. This time it wasn't a placeholder kiss.

He was startled for just a second. She could taste his surprise, feel that instant of hesitation. Then it was gone and he was kissing her back, and they were kissing as if they'd die otherwise. Mouth to mouth, chest to breast, groin to groin. He was hard, grinding against her and her legs opened naturally so she could feel him right ... there. Oh God, red-hot lightning shot through her as she lifted herself up so she could rub against him better.

Her open sex rubbed against the satiny lining of her dress.

She felt it the instant he realized what she realized. She wasn't wearing panties and there was absolutely nothing between her vagina and Cal's penis but some material to be lifted and unzipped. She could feel the heat of him rubbing against her and pressed against him even harder.

He backed her against the wall and she could feel crumbling bits of brick dust showering her, floating to the ground. His weight against her felt so good, as hard as the brick wall behind her. He kissed her and kissed her and kissed her, one hand holding her head, the other dropping to her silk dress, with hardly any beads left on it.

He was pulling the skirt up when they heard the voices.

Two bass voices.

Where the fuck did they go?

Dunno. Call the others.

In English. American English.

She looked startled at Cal. They had *Americans* after them? Why?

Then: *Alert Morris. We need more manpower.* The sounds of bootsteps, walking quickly down the calle.

"Those were Americans," Anya said breathlessly, voice low. It was hard to wrap her head around that. "And did you hear that name? Do you think it might be Ash Morris?"

That was why the American who'd threatened her at Palazzo Maltese seemed so familiar. She'd met Ash Morris once, very briefly. But she'd disliked him on sight and he'd remained in her memory.

Cal kept his voice very low, too. "Yeah. The fucker asked about you at the party. Wanted me to find you. Then he put a tracker in my jacket." He looked at her, face tight with anger. It came off him in waves. "They got to you through me. It's all my fault —"

She shook her head sharply. "Don't go there. This isn't your fault. If anything it's Ash Morris's fault. He's with the US Embassy in Beirut but actually —"

"He's CIA," Cal finished.

How did Cal — she looked at him. He was an engineer through and through. A man of technology and science. He'd never been interested in politics but she imagined that he had a good grasp of the geopolitics behind the Accords and would know the major players. Ash Morris had never been in the forefront but he'd definitely been pulling strings in the background.

Just not for his country, apparently.

"We need to get you squared away." Cal put a little distance between them and she immediately missed him.

Missed his hardness and heat. In his arms, it was as if he'd been able to lend her his strength. But now that he wasn't touching her, she realized just how weak she was. She sagged, saved from falling by his strong hand on her arm.

"I'm fine," she murmured but he wasn't listening. He was looking intently at the door to the repair shop. It was an ancient shop, with two front windows completely covered by thick wooden shutters. The door was made of even thicker wood, with bronze rivets and hinges. Inside there was no doubt a thick wooden bar besides the brand new deadbolt lock.

"Goddamn," he whispered. "Left my lockpick set in the hotel. Last time that will ever happen."

He eyed the door more carefully, checked out into the passageway, then stepped back. He was going to try to kick the door in. He would undoubtedly be able to do it, but it would take several tries and they'd make a huge noise.

Plus, she knew from experience that though the street looked deserted, there were dozens of flats above the shops. Venetians, the real kind, the original residents, were few and dwindling. The ones that were left in the city looked after each other. Someone would call the police. That wasn't a bad thing but if they were taken into custody, they could be trapped. There could be an army after them. If they were willing to kidnap her, shock her, torture her, who knows what else they'd be willing to do? And who knew how high it went? Maybe they were allied with people in positions of power.

Cal lifted his foot to try to bash the door in, but she stopped him with a hand on his arm.

"These doors have been here for hundreds of years. And they are probably reinforced with steel bars on the inside. I think I know where we can go until your cavalry arrives." She had to put a hand out to the wall for a second.

Cal wrapped his big hand around her arm again. "As long as it's close by. You're too weak to walk far. I can carry you but then I won't be able to react if we run into those fuckheads."

She closed her eyes. She'd been here with one of the secretaries, an Italian friend who worked at Peace and Jobs. Marcella had studied in Venice and knew it inside out. She was the one who'd suggested the umbrella repair shop. They'd gone ... Anya put the heels of her hands against her eyes, trying to focus. There was static in her head, her mind a radio station she couldn't tune into.

She pressed the heels of her hands harder into her eyes, focusing. She could feel Cal next to her, waiting. He didn't say anything, didn't try to push her. He knew she was trying hard.

They could be gunned down at any moment and she was trapping them here because she couldn't ... *think.*

Some noise must have escaped her because he gathered her up against him, warm and solid and safe.

"I can't remember," she whispered. "There's something, but I can't remember!"

"Shhh," he whispered back, bending low, his lips touching her ear. She shivered as a blast of heat shot through her, blowing away the fog in her head. "It's okay."

Anya pushed against him, just a little. Not that she wanted to get away from him but because he needed room to maneuver in. She stood on tiptoe to put her lips against his ear.

"I just remembered." Pulling back she looked into his eyes, placing a finger against her lips.

He nodded and stepped back, holding her by the arms. Ready to let her take charge, but supporting her.

Tears welled in her eyes. That was how they'd been, that was how they'd operated, all those years ago. Whoever was best at something did it and the other was there for support.

She'd never had that before and had never had it since.

His eyes widened as he saw her eyes welling and she shook her head fiercely, angry at herself. This was no time to get emotional.

Cocking an ear at the calle where the men had run past, she waited another moment. No one was running by. Though the men after them could be anywhere, they had to make their move now. They had to get to some kind of shelter, now.

Anya grabbed Cal's hand, feeling an infusion of strength and heat. Where they were going wasn't far. She didn't want him to have to carry her. She just had to suck it up, the pain and the aching muscles and the trembling.

He pulled gently, bent again to her ear. "Can you walk?"

No, but she had to. No choice. She gave him a trembling smile and quoted one of their favorite movie lines. "Ain't got time to bleed."

And lead him out of the passageway and into another calle. This one ran alongside a canal. She knew more or less where she was in the city but right now she was running on memory. She'd been with Marcella and they'd taken a lunchtime stroll and ... yes. There was that ochre yellow house on the canal that had particularly pretty geranium boxes. And — yep — further down a tiny little charming square with a coffee shop with three tables out where they'd stopped for a cappuccino. The coffee shop was closed but she recognized it. Then they'd strolled further down, crossed a bridge and — yes!

There it was! One of the many *stazioni gondola* dotting the city's canals. The 400 gondolas that plied the lagoon by day had all to come to rest like birds at night and this was one of their nesting places.

And not a moment too soon because Anya felt her knees start to shake. She held herself up by sheer will as she pointed to the striped pole with five gondolas tied up.

"There," she said. "Lots of gondolas are covered with tarps. Maybe we might find one and hole up in the bottom of the hull until the cavalry arrives."

"Good thinking," Cal murmured, putting his hand around her waist. She needed it. She was shaking all over and though he saw it — hell, he could feel it — he didn't say anything.

The calle was above the banks of the canal. There were steps running down to the bank and the gondolas. Cal wrapped her hand around the railing, hopped down and held his hands up. Anya leaned forward, utterly certain that he'd catch her.

He did.

Around a corner came the sounds of boot heels, running. It was impossible to tell how far away they were. Sounds did strange things in this city, bouncing off the narrow streets and canals.

He half carried her to the middle gondola, slightly larger, with a tied-down tarp covering the inside. Cal untied one section, helped her under it, got under himself, then pulled the tarp over them, tying it loosely.

There would be no way to tell that they were there.

"Let's hope they don't have IR goggles," Cal whispered in her ear.

Oh, God, so there *would* be a way to tell that they were there.

"Doubt it, though," he added. "I didn't see anything like that, did you? They had night vision but not the kind that has IR capability."

Anya ran her head back over her captivity. She'd been frightened and angry and frankly, not noticing much. The man who'd shocked her hadn't had anything in his hand other than the electric prod. He'd been armed though. Some kind of gun in a shoulder holster. The two guards had been empty handed, too, other than their weapons. Everything spoke of an operation set up hastily, and of course they thought they'd be dealing with an unarmed woman. Which they had, of course. Fuckers hadn't counted on Cal being in the mix.

Cal settled her along the velvet-lined bottom of the gondola, shoving the two chairs to either side of the narrow area, so that the tarp was slightly lifted. It wasn't how gondolas were stored but Anya didn't imagine the goons would know that.

The floor was narrow. The velvet smelled of feet and mold, though if it hid them, she couldn't complain. The water in the canal was still, placid, but there was a feeling of buoyancy.

She lay on her side, front facing the open water and could feel Cal settling in behind her. It was a tight fit but they managed. He'd taken his tuxedo jacket off and tucked it under her head so she'd be more comfortable.

He put his lips to her ear. "Are you okay?"

She shivered. He was like a warm, living wall at her back,

one big arm around her waist. He was curved around her and she knew, like she knew that the sun was going to rise in the east tomorrow morning, that he was angling himself so he would catch any bullet first.

Cal nudged her with his shoulder. "Anya?"

Her voice came out husky. "I'm ok."

He pulled his cell from the inside pocket of his tux jacket under her head and switched it on. It required his thumbprint and then a six character code. Once it was on, he switched on an app Anya didn't recognize. From the same inside jacket pocket he fished out a wireless ear bud and fixed it in one ear.

The screen was very bright — the scene of Petra at dawn.

"Cal," she murmured, "dim the light."

"God yes." The cell screen dimmed to almost blackness. "Sorry. Little preoccupied here."

She smiled over her shoulder at him.

He thumbed a saved number and pressed, bringing the phone to his mouth. It was picked up immediately. She could only hear his end of the conversation, barely making out the words even though his mouth was an inch from her ear.

"New intel. Two of the guys after us are Americans. Probably Ash Morris's, though I don't know whether they are freelancers or Christians in Action." He listened. "Yeah. Listen, get reinforcements. Good ones. Armed. You know where we are. I switched on the tracker. You have the GPS."

He put the cell back in the inside pocket together with the wireless bud. "So my guy is still fifteen minutes out. He thought he'd be here by now. He's in a private boat but he said the Canal is overcrowded and he's going to have to dock at St. Mark's Square and cross it on foot and that it's wall-to-wall revellers. He estimates another fifteen minutes, like I said, but he's calling in the troops."

"Who would the troops be?"

"Farris is well-connected. It might be the Carabinieri, might be the Polizia di Stato. Might be a good local security team. If that's the case, though, we're still going to the cops."

Anya nodded. They were getting out of this nightmare. "They wanted to know about my friend June Chen."

Cal hooked his chin on her shoulder, cheek rubbing against hers. He had a little sandy stubble already. She'd loved it when he wore his scruffy look, light stubble over tanned skin.

It had been a long long time since she'd felt his whiskers rubbing her cheek.

Cal turned his head to look at her. "Who's June Chen?"

"A really good friend. She's Chinese American, family came over twenty years ago when she was a kid. Father's super smart, an astrophysicist, mom's a concert pianist. Brother's a biochemist, sister is an orthopedic surgeon. She's the underachiever in the family, she studied journalism at Harvard. She's on the China desk at the New York Times, digital edition. I think she might have sent me a text or a video. As soon as we're clear, we need to switch on my cell. We can ..." her voice trailed off as he pulled her cell from his pants pocket, put in the battery and SIM card and switched it on.

"You have Petra as a screensaver too," Cal said absently. She turned her head and their eyes met and it was as if a current had switched on between them. She nodded, not trusting her voice.

Call pulled out another wireless ear bud, handing it to her along with her cell. She went to the right app.

"I noticed you don't even have password protection." She could hear the heavy disapproval in his voice. Anya sighed.

"It's my private one. My work cell is password protected." He gave her a sideways fulminating glance out of narrowed eyes. "Okay okay," she whispered. "Total password protection from now on, on all my devices."

"Randomly generated, switched out every couple of weeks."

She rolled her eyes, sighed and nodded. He was right. She didn't like it that he was right, but he was. Cal had always been security conscious. Clearly, running a billion dollar business hadn't improved things.

"Yes."

"Promise."

She sighed again. "Yes, I promise."

"I don't really need that promise because I will personally make sure you do that. After tonight I don't think I'll let you out of my sight again."

A burst of heat and joy bloomed in her chest. The idea of Cal scolding her for a long, long time about passwords made her ridiculously happy. He didn't even seem to realize the implications of what he'd said. He nudged her shoulder with his own. "Let's see what your friend says."

Anya thumbed the app and — oh my God! — There she was! June! Her best friend. The image was grainy and the sound was bad, and June was whispering. But what she was saying was clear.

Her pretty, scared face filled the screen. She kept looking over her shoulder. "Anya, I'm sending this to you first. I can't send it to my editor because I need more corroboration. But I need to tell you that there's going to be an attempt in

Venice on Hu Lin's life tomorrow some time before the signing ceremony."

Anya's breath caught in her throat. A chill spread through her body. She knew *exactly* what that meant.

"You're more familiar with the political aspects of the Accords. I'm assuming that this would have a profound effect on them." Cal's low voice was in her ear as she stopped the recording.

Anya tilted her head toward him. "Not a profound effect. It would bring the Accords to a grinding halt. They would fail and it would take another decade to put them back together again. Except the Accords failing would not leave things as they were, bad as that was. The Accords failing could very well mean world war, and I don't mean like World War II. I mean war throughout the world, east against west, north against south. Everyone fighting everyone else."

"How's that? I mean these Accords have been years in the making. How could the death of one man change all that?"

"Not just one man. This one man." Anya's fingers curled the cell. Her muscles hurt, everything hurt, and now her heart hurt. "The Accords are built on the safeguards guaranteed by the six main signatories. The US, the UK, France, Russia, Saudi Arabia and China."

Cal nodded, clearly still not understanding.

"If one of the Six Pillars crumbles, the entire edifice crumbles, that is built into the Accords. If Hu Lin dies, the man who is next in succession is a rabid China Firster. He will pull out of the Accords immediately and would be happy to do it spectacularly, the day the Accords are supposed to be signed. And everything will go up in smoke. He'd like nothing more than to wreck the whole process."

"Fuck," Cal muttered.

"About sums it up," she agreed.

"Let's watch the rest," he said.

She thumbed the video back on and June's frozen face became animated again. "I'm going to keep digging in Beijing and see if I can come up with enough concrete info to publish. There's some evidence that an American who works for the CIA might be involved, too, which would be a disaster. Li Wei, who would succeed Hu Lin, would pay big bucks to anyone who helped trash the Accords. Anyway, you're on the scene. Pass this on to anyone you think might be able to protect Hu Lin. If it's a false alarm, no harm done. If it's not, we might be able to save the Accords from failing. I'm going to be hard to find the next few days. Check our message board."

The video stopped, frozen on June's worried and scared face.

"We need to contact someone," Anya said. "Someone with the power to protect Hu Lin."

Cal didn't answer. He tapped the first number on his contacts list again and brought the cell to his lips, speaking in a voice so low she could barely follow. "Yo, it's me." He listened for a moment. "We seem to be well hidden for the moment. Listen, there's something new. It looks like this whole thing, including that fuckhead Ash, is about a possible attempt on the life of the President of China, Hu Lin." He listened. "Yeah. Do you know anyone you trust in Italian law enforcement? Yeah. Excellent. Call him. Get an extra security detail around Hu. See you in fifteen."

Cal put the cell back in his inside jacket pocket and settled back down, wrapping her in his big arms.

He nosed aside a lock of her hair and whispered in her ear. "How are we feeling?"

Oh God. His breath against her ear provoked a shiver all along her body. He knew perfectly well how much her ears were erogenous zones, though only with him, she found later. One lover had tried to drill a hole in her ear with his tongue, saliva dribbling, and it had creeped her out. She'd had to jerk her head away.

But not Cal. The feel of his warm breath, the sound of his low voice, shot heat through her.

It was almost frightening the power Cal had over her body, as if it didn't entirely belong to her but partly belonged to him, too. As it had when they were young.

She tried to keep her voice light. "I don't know about you, but I'm feeling all right. Better, at any rate."

It was true, she realized. Lying in Cal's arms, feeling his body next to hers — almost around hers — shot heat and strength through her. She'd employed the oldest trick in the world while being tortured. The one she'd turned to instinctively though she knew soldiers were taught it as a technique — distancing herself from her body. She'd flown right out of it and hadn't come back fully yet, until now.

But here she was. Her body ached, was sore. She was exhausted. But she was in it, a part of it, and that was all because of Cal.

How long had it been since she'd lain with someone like this? Feeling a body against her back, so close she could feel the rise and fall of his chest, his breath tickling her hair?

A long, long time. She'd had a few sex partners, but she didn't cuddle after sex. Didn't sleep in anyone's arms. In bed, she was all business and once that business was over, she was out of bed and dressing or in the shower hoping the guy du jour would be gone by the time she came out.

This felt like surrender, the best kind of surrender. She could let herself go because Cal would catch her.

"I think we're safe here," he murmured. Though he had a deep voice, she was sure they couldn't possibly be heard up on the street.

"I think so too." And because she felt safe for the first time since those men kidnapped her at Palazzo Maltese, she was able to focus on the bigger danger. The danger to the world. "Do you think your friend can mobilize the troops?"

"I don't know about the troops, but Farris is friends with someone high up in the Polizia. I think they cross-trained. The other guy is special ops, too, or was. It's a fraternity. Unless they've already whacked the Chinese President, he is now going to be protected."

"Thank God." She closed her eyes. "I'm so glad I was with you. I don't know if I'd have known who to call, who to contact. I might have lost time or even, God forbid, contacted the wrong people. Made things worse."

His arms tightened around her. "Damned right it's a good thing you're with me. I told you before, I'm not letting you out of my sight." He buried his face in her neck. "Right now, I don't think I can let you get far enough away that I can't touch you."

She smiled. Closed her hand around his. "That works out just fine. Because I want to be close enough to touch you, too."

He tensed. Lifted his face from her neck. "Yeah?"

"Yeah."

"I meant that — what's the word? Not literally."

"Metaphorically."

One hand dropped down to the hem of her dress and

began sliding upwards, bringing heat with it. "Yeah. Metaphorically. I meant that metaphorically."

His hand was sliding up her thigh. He reached the top of her thigh-highs, lingering.

"Mm." Anya felt heat all through her. Her lungs were on fire. It was hard to talk. She swallowed. "I didn't."

"Hmm?" Cal moved, covered her mound with his hand. She was completely naked, open to him. He waggled his hand and she opened her thighs. He kissed her ear and she shivered. "You didn't what?"

"Mean it metaphorically."

Cal's hand slid over her sex, one finger outlining her opening. Anya could barely breathe. She moved her hips in time with his finger, wanting to be touched ...

"God. I can't follow. Mind's blasted." His voice in her ear was low and hoarse.

Right ...

"I want you to touch me," she said breathlessly. "All the time. In every way." Anya took his hand, put her finger over his and positioned it ...

There!

Cal circled his finger, with just exactly the right kind of pressure, as if he knew her body perfectly. Which, of course, he did. He dipped his head and caught her ear lobe between his teeth and bit lightly, delicately, but firmly. Like a stallion nips his mare. Just as he entered her with two fingers.

Anya convulsed, clenching around his fingers, her body out of her control in a white hot fever of pleasure so intense it wiped out the memory of the torture. Pain was a thing of the past, what existed now was pure pleasure, her sex clenching tightly around his hand.

She drew in a deep breath because the pleasure had to

express itself somehow and his hand covered her mouth. "No noise," he whispered.

Oh God. No of course she couldn't make any noise. For just a second she forgot *why* she couldn't make noise, why she couldn't express her pleasure with a cry and the ban made it somehow more intense. With no release other than that of her body, it became deeper and hotter, these tiny convulsions deep inside her.

Cal held her tightly through it, curling his body even more closely around hers, judging the moment when he could lift his hand from her mouth. She was breathing fast, but remained perfectly silent.

"That's my girl." He kissed the side of her face. "I'm so —"

The sounds of running feet, men's voices, harsh and low.

Anya stiffened and Cal loosened his hold on her.

"Cal!" A male voice called out.

"Yo," he said, unhooked the tarp and stood up. "We're here."

10

The possible assassination of the President of China and the possible cancellation of the Mediterranean Accords were a Big Deal. Cal was an engineer but he wasn't a dummy. Thousands and thousands of people had worked hundreds of thousands of hours on this and billions of dollars had been spent. One billion was going to flow into his own bank account.

But that meant less to him than the fact that Anya was barely able to stand upright on her feet. He had long ago passed the point where more money meant anything to him. He had enough for ten lifetimes. What was important was the woman at his side.

Farris had brought a few guys from the Phoenix security team and they had brought a couple of Polizia di Stato officers and a few soldiers kitted out in full commando gear. The soldiers and Farris's guys stood in a semicircle on the calle level, backs to them, weapons trained, eyes front while Cal flipped back the tarp covering the passenger part of the gondola and helped Anya out.

It hadn't been easy not making love to her on that smelly gondola carpet. He should be given some kind of medal for his self restraint. But it was worth it because though her face was drawn, and she was a little shaky, there was color in her face again. Just a little rosiness under the skin that was pale from fatigue and pain.

If he could give her that moment's pleasure, man it was worth it. And they'd have plenty of time for real sex. The rest of their lives, in fact.

But for the moment, there was still business to attend to.

She was putting up a brave front but her hand trembled and her jaw was clenched. Goddamn. He tried to put his arm around her but she gave a subtle shake of her head and took his arm, as if they were at some goddamned ball.

She needed his arm and leaned heavily on him, but it looked better than him half holding her up.

It flashed on him what her role had been, a woman negotiating peace in a man's world, where everyone hated everyone else.

Never show weakness. That clearly had been drummed into her. Never show weakness, always put up a strong front.

He wanted to say that it wasn't necessary. These were his men and Italian police officers and soldiers. No one would think less of her if she showed weakness and if they did, Cal would punch their lights out.

But she was adamant that she wanted to walk under her own steam as much as possible, head held high.

Farris walked by his side and the Phoenix men surrounded them, the Italian officers forming a looser perimeter, one taking point, one taking up the rear. The soldiers had melted into the background but Cal knew they were there.

"I want to get Anya to a safe place where she can rest. She's been tortured." Cal shot a glance at Farris and saw his jaw tighten.

"Fuck," Farris said softly and Cal shook his head at him, frowning. The fuck? You didn't say fuck in front of a fucking lady.

"Sorry." Farris dipped his head.

"You can say fuck, whoever you are. It's very apt. It wasn't pleasant." Anya was shaking but her voice was steady.

Cal indicated Farris by backhanding his chest. Not gently. "Anya, this is my head of security, Joe Farris. Joe, Anya Voronova —"

"Deputy Director of Peace and Jobs," Farris said smoothly. He stuck his head a little forward and spoke across Cal. "Very pleased to meet you. You guys did good work on the Accords."

"Thank you." Anya gave a slight smile.

Cal shot him A Look.

"What?" Farris shrugged. "Unlike you, I paid attention to more than the technical issues. That's what you pay me for, to be informed. While you were in the desert studying pipelines, these guys got down and dirty with the negotiations. So, hats off. Whoa."

She'd stumbled. Cal put his arm around her waist and glared at Farris who'd put a hand out. Glaring at Farris was a total dick move and Cal knew it but he couldn't help it.

No one was touching Anya but him.

Farris held his hands up. *Not touching her.*

Luckily Anya missed him being a fuckhead but Farris sure didn't.

"The police are waiting for your statement, Dr. Voronova.

We're headed for the *Questura*, Police Headquarters, which is right —"

Cal stiffened, turning his head to Farris. "Man, let's not do this now. Anya's been kidnapped and tortured and I'm not going to have her be subjected —"

"Cal." He whipped his head around to see her beautiful, aggravated face. She pushed away from him a little, removing his arm from her waist, pushing her hand into the crook of his elbow again. "This thing is bigger than the two of us and certainly bigger than any tiredness I might feel. My friend June might be in trouble, and the Accords are definitely in trouble. If they break down right on the eve of signing, the world will become even more dangerous than it already is. It would be catastrophic. There'd be a degree of distrust that would be like a powder keg just waiting to blow up." She looked across Cal at Farris, nodding her head. "Of course we're headed for the Questura and I am taking it as a given that security around Hu has been ramped up."

"Absolutely. As a matter of fact, I am told that he is now in a secure location. I don't know where and I bet there are only a few people who do know. I also know that he'll be taken to the Doge's Palace for the signing tomorrow under the tightest security that can be devised. Trust me, no one wants the Accords derailed."

They turned a corner. Phoenix Security operatives — men he knew and trusted — had already been around the corner and given the all clear. There, about a hundred feet down a sizeable street for Venice, around fifteen feet across, was a little square with a building at the end of it. The building was squat and red and had *QVESTVRA*, in old-timey Roman script, written across the façade in big brass letters.

Sounds of revelry came from far off but the square itself was empty. It took Cal a moment to remember that it was still the night of Mardi Gras. It felt like a century had gone by.

The road and the square had been cleared of any civilians. Soldiers lined the street. Hard-eyed, submachine guns at port arms, fingers lying alongside the triggers. Those fingers would be inside the trigger guards at the faintest sound of danger.

Cal glanced at Anya and she had on her grim effort face, the one she'd had when she aced her philology test though she'd studied through the flu and a temperature of 101°. There'd been no talking her out of it then, and he sighed to himself as he realized there was no talking her out of this now.

So — he was going to help her.

"Come on honey," he said as they approached the steps up to the narrow glass doors of the entrance.

She gave him a sideways glance. "You're not going to try to talk me out of it?"

"Would it do any good? Me trying to talk you out of this?"

"Nope."

He gave an exaggerated sigh. "Well, then." And stretched out a hand, *After you*. They couldn't go through together, it wasn't wide enough. But right past the doors, he took her arm.

The Italian security detail remained outside the glass doors, but Farris and the Phoenix operators came through. Inside the marble-lined lobby there was a man waiting for them in a gray suit, with gray hair and gray eyes and an unmistakable aura of power. Institutional power.

Cal was familiar with the type. He'd dealt mainly with

Energy and Infrastructure Ministers but he'd also dealt with his share of top cops. The desalination plants were destiny-changers in many countries and their security was a top priority.

The man sized them all up in one cool glance, instantly separating the security forces, including Farris, from Anya and him. Then, in a microsecond, figuring out who was most important, discarding him, and zooming in on Anya.

Impressive.

He walked toward Anya, not waiting for her to come to him. "Doctor Voronova, a pleasure. I am Vincenzo Ambrosini, the Questore of Venice." He offered a hand that was callused, very odd in a man who was wearing a suit worth a couple thousand bucks. "I understand you are Deputy Director of Peace and Jobs. Your NGO has done excellent work."

Anya straightened, visibly trying not to sway.

"Dr. Ambrosini," she said. She tightened her left hand on Cal's arm while extending her right hand.

Nothing escaped the chief of police's notice. He stepped back and swept his hand toward a marble-floored hallway. "Please, let us sit down. I understand you had quite an ordeal. Let me lead the way."

Farris came with them as they trooped down the corridor to the big wooden door at the end of the hallway. The Questore opened the door and ushered them in. Several very comfortable looking chairs were arranged in a semicircle around a big, elaborately-carved keyhole desk.

"Please," he said, indicating the chairs. "I'll order us some coffee. Four espressos?"

Cal had pushed two of the chairs together so they were

touching, helped Anya sit down, then sat down himself. Anya smiled. "I'd love some tea, if I may."

The Questore looked utterly blank. As if the concept of tea were foreign. Manners, however, won out. "Of course. I'm sure we have a tea bag somewhere." He stuck his head out of the door, gave an order in liquid Italian, then closed it and sat behind his desk, steepling his fingers.

"Dr. Voronova, I understand full well how exhausted you are, but —"

"This is a time-sensitive issue, Dr. Ambrosini," Anya said, her voice a little firmer. "My exhaustion has nothing to do with it. Lives hang in the balance, not to mention the fact that the Accords are at stake."

The Questore's grey eyes turned stony. "The Accords. Losing the Accords would be a tragedy."

"Yes." She narrowed her eyes until only a dot of glowing pale blue showed. "That's not going to happen."

"No, Doctor," he replied, "that's not going to happen. It would be a disaster, possibly ending in war. Excuse me." He rose at the soft knock at the door.

A uniformed officer walked in carrying a tray with three espressos and a cappuccino cup with a white paper square on a string coming out of it. Her tea. The water wasn't hot and the tea bag was turning it a pale yellow color like piss. Cal was really glad he'd gone for the espresso.

The Questore sat back behind his desk. "First of all, I'd like you to know that the President of China is now in a secure place under armed guard. So, Dr. Voronova, do you want to tell me what happened?"

Cal watched her carefully. She was very pale and looked stressed but other than that she was composed, voice steady.

It was impossible to tell that not an hour ago she'd been tortured.

"I was at the reception this evening at Palazzo Maltese, representing Peace and Jobs since my boss had a meeting in Cairo. He'll be arriving tomorrow —" she glanced at her watch. It was two am. "Today. The reception was a little boring and I was tired. At around 8 p.m. I went up to the second floor — first floor to you. I knew speeches would be starting around nine but I thought I'd sit and rest for a while. While there, I saw Cal." She looked at him, gave a faint smile. "Calvin Burns. Head of Phoenix Enterprises. We knew each other in college but hadn't seen each other for ten years."

Her voice was cool, collected. No one could possibly know that they'd fucked like minks. Not by tone of voice or a flicker of eyes in his direction or change of color. She'd spent years on diplomatic missions and it showed. She was very good.

"While we were talking, catching up on old times, we both received text messages at the same time. It had been prearranged that texts would be sent out to the main parties when it was time for the family photo."

Cal knew — because he'd been told — that the family photo at big events frequented by politicians was a photo of all the participants and it was that photo that went into the history books.

Frankly, Cal didn't give a shit about the history books.

The Questore looked at him, head cocked. Was he supposed to say something? "Our phones got mixed up."

Anya smoothly glided over how their phones got mixed up. "The lights went out. That was when several men broke into the room where we were talking. It was a blur. I could hear the sounds of fighting. Cal brought down two of the men, then they sprayed him with a gas. It smelled like chloroform. I could see that he was down when they switched on the flashlight function of their cells. They forced me to wear one of those Venetian porcelain masks but with no eyeholes and no nose holes for breathing. When I hesitated to put it on, one of the men punched me in the stomach, then stuck a gun in my side. They made it clear that if I called for help they'd shoot."

They'd punched her in the stomach? What the hell? That was the first he'd heard of it. Of course he'd been lying unconscious on the floor.

"What?" Cal had been completely thrown by the image of Anya doubled over from a punch in the stomach. He wished he could go back and break the rest of their bones. His head buzzed with rage.

"How many men?" the Questore asked him. Cal realized he was asking for the second time. He had to shake his head to come back into the moment.

"Four or five, I'd say. Remember it was dark. I fought two of them off."

"Mr. Burns has a black belt in judo and is a fourth dan," Farris said helpfully.

"A knowledge of martial arts isn't much of a help when you're being chloroformed," Cal said.

"Indeed not." Mr. Ambrosini's mouth tightened. "Then what happened?" He addressed Anya.

"I wasn't chloroformed but I was incapacitated. I could barely breath, because of the punch and because the mask was so tight. I thought for a moment I was going to suffocate, until I learned that if I breathed in a shallow manner, I would be okay. Then I realized they were taking me somewhere. If they wanted me somewhere else that meant they didn't want me dead. Not right away, anyway."

"This wasn't the first time you'd been kidnapped," Ambrosini said.

"No." Anya shuddered. "It isn't."

Cal turned his head and looked at her. It felt like his chest was going to explode, his eyeballs burst out of his head. His Anya had been kidnapped before?

When? Who?

The fuck?

She didn't pick up on the violent emotions running through him. A slender shoulder rose and fell on a shrug. "In the fall of 2019. I was kidnapped by a breakaway faction of Hamas who didn't want any part of the peace negotiations. Luckily, I was ransomed immediately. I just hoped that this group — whoever it was — was as greedy as that other group."

Her voice turned hoarse. "I was so worried about Cal, though I could see he was breathing before they put the mask on me."

"What language were they speaking?"

"Chinese. Mandarin. And they spoke like soldiers, using military terminology. But the man who held a gun to my side spoke English to me. And there had been another man, who entered the room briefly. In costume. He sounded American. But the others were Chinese."

"You speak Chinese." It wasn't a question.

She dipped her head. "I do. Both Mandarin and Cantonese and I've spent enough time in China to be able to understand a number of dialects. But these men didn't speak any dialect nor did they speak with a regional accent. Like I said, they talked like soldiers. Even if they weren't active-duty soldiers, they'd had military training. They came prepared to kidnap me." She shot Cal a Look. "Settle down."

He'd half risen from his seat, unable to control himself. He felt Farris's heavy hand on his shoulder and subsided. Ashamed of himself.

Sort of.

Mr. Ambrosini looked from Anya to him and back. Whatever he was thinking, nothing showed on his face. "What did they want from you?"

Anya sighed. "Well, that's the thing. Nothing I could give them. They wanted to know when was the last time I spoke with June Chen."

"The journalist?" Mr. Ambrosini cocked his head. Cal was really impressed. He'd never heard of June Chen until an hour ago.

"Yes. They questioned me over and over about the last time I spoke with her. The last time I spoke with June was in Istanbul at the Decision Makers Conference last November. And it was an informal meeting between friends."

"They didn't believe you?"

"They didn't. The man questioning me was insistent that a conversation between the two of us had been overheard at noon today. Yesterday, actually. He kept saying that June had spoken to me. I think they realized then that she'd called me and maybe left a message. So they wanted me to access my messages on my cell."

"But it wasn't her cell, it was mine," Cal said.

Anya nodded. "We had identical cells and I'd put his in my purse by mistake."

Cal was watching Anya carefully and again marveled at her ability to present a façade that gave nothing away. She was a born diplomat.

"When I saw it wasn't mine and that it was password protected, I knew I had to stall. I couldn't give them what they wanted and I was afraid —" her voice caught on the word, the first sign of emotion she'd shown. Her long, pale throat bobbed as she swallowed. When she spoke she was again in complete control. "I was afraid that if they discovered I couldn't give them any information, they'd kill me. And then go after Cal. So I — resisted, I guess you'd say."

"They fucking tortured her," Cal said heatedly. Unlike her he couldn't keep emotion out of his voice. They'd *tortured* Anya and if he could go back and kill them all slowly and painfully, he'd do it. "They can't get away with it."

"They surely won't, Dr. Burns," Ambrosini said, tone cold. "We do not allow that here in Venice."

"The man who — who interrogated me used a stun gun. Something like a cattle prod, which delivered an electric shock when it touched skin. It — it felt very powerful. I think —" she cleared her throat. "I think if they'd continued long enough, my heart would have given out."

"Meaning kill you," Ambrosini said.

"Yes." Anya looked at Cal then away again. He knew what his face looked like. He looked like death and he was. Coming for the fuckers who'd tortured her. "Yes. It was a waiting game. How long I could hold out. How much patience they had. Their timeline seemed to be tight. I knew I had to hold out until Cal could come."

She held out her hand and he took it, brought her hand to his mouth. Didn't care who saw it.

Ambrosini switched his attention to Cal. It was like coming under a spotlight. Not a particularly pleasant sensation.

"So, Dr. Burns. You saved her. How did you find her?"

Cal didn't mention the beads. "It was my cell she took with her. A company cell. We have an app on all our phones so we can be tracked when we're in the field. We are used to working in uncharted desert environments and dangerous urban environments. The app tracks in real time and to an accuracy of one meter. I followed the app to a warehouse. Where I found four men guarding an abandoned building that looked like a warehouse and one man interrogating Dr. Voronova ..."

He stopped, throat constricted, unable to continue.

Anya squeezed his arm, and picked up the story. She'd always been able to read him. "Cal arrived just in time. I don't know how much longer I'd have been able to hold out. He managed to incapacitate the men and get me out. We hid in a gondola at one of the *stazioni* until his men and some of your officers came to get us. In the meantime, I was able to check my phone to see what they were trying to get from me. I found a message from June Chen. They must have over-heard her leaving it for me. I think she's in Athens at the moment. June found out there was going to be an attempt on the life of the President of China here in Venice, before the signing of the —"

Everyone's phone went off, buzzing and pulsing and ringing. Every single one.

Cal checked his screen. PRESIDENT OF CHINA SAFE. Sent by one of Farris's men. He met Farris's eyes.

Mr. Ambrosini reached out and clicked on the keyboard of the giant monitor on his desk. He turned it around so they could see. It was a channel called RAI NEWS, RAI being the state channel of Italy.

A red chyron was scrolling across the bottom of the

screen. SVENTATO ATTENTATO ALLA VITA DEL PRESIDENTE DELLA CINA.

Anya turned to him. "An attack on the life of the President of China has just been thwarted."

He smiled at her. "Italian, too?"

She shrugged. She was a genius with languages, his princess.

Ambrosini was shifting his attention between the screen and his phone. He was the chief law enforcement officer in the city, his phone was telling him more than the state broadcasting company was telling them.

He read off his phone. "Three men were arrested outside the hotel suite where President Hu was staying. His bodyguards had been incapacitated and the video cameras switched off. But thanks to the extra security added at the last minute —" He looked up from his phone screen and gave a grateful nod to Cal, Anya and Farris, "President Hu is in a safe location and has stated that he will be at the signing ceremony."

Cal leaned forward. "I have reason to believe that an American was involved, probably for money. His name is Ashley Morris. He was CIA, might not be at the moment. But he was neck-deep in it."

"How do you know, Dr. Burns?" Ambrosini asked. "Are you certain? Accusing the CIA of what would be treason is a serious business."

"I'm not accusing the CIA, I'm accusing one operative and whoever was working with him."

Cal pulled out the tiny tracker he'd found in his jacket pocket, placed it on the highly polished surface of Ambrosini's desk. "Tracker. Found it in my pocket. Ash placed it there. He was at the reception looking for Dr. Voronova. All he had to identify her with was a copy of her Peace and Jobs badge photograph. He said that he had facial recognition software in his cell, but it was a masked ball. If Anya — Dr. Voronova — was wearing a mask it couldn't work. So he saw me and asked if I could find Anya for him. He knew we were friends in college. And he must have put the tracker in my pocket then. So the kidnapers knew exactly where to find her."

Mr. Ambrosini turned the tracker over with the tip of a pencil. "Too small to take fingerprints."

"Yeah." Cal leaned forward. "But I'd be willing to testify in any court in the world that he was the one who slipped it into my pocket."

Though Cal hadn't seen it, he'd cheerfully perjure himself if it could be one brick in the wall that incarcerated Ash Morris.

It still burned that he'd been an instrument of the bad guys finding Anya. If he hadn't been blasted by the idea of seeing her after ten years, he'd have figured it out sooner. And then seeing Anya — every thought in his head had just disappeared, like fog in the wind.

Ambrosini was taking notes in a notebook.

Anya's eyes closed and didn't open again. She was slumping up against him. Well, she'd saved the Mediterranean Accords, changed the course of history. She deserved to rest. Cal rose.

"Mr. Ambrosini, if there are no further questions, I'm taking Dr. Voronova to the closest medical facility and then making sure she rests."

Anya came to with a start. "Oh! No! Cal, I'm fine."

He deliberately looked her up and down, not in a lover-like gaze but assessing her. She looked exhausted, completely drained. "You're not fine. You've been manhandled and punched and terrorized and tortured. A doctor should look at you."

She shook her head and to his alarm, That Look he recognized came over that beautiful face. It was the look of when she could not be swayed.

"I don't want a doctor, I don't want a medical center, I want a shower and a bed and I want to be there for the ceremony tomorrow. Peace and Jobs has worked tirelessly for this and I will be there."

Fuck. When she decided something, that was it. He knew that. Cal gave up, but not with grace.

"Where is your hotel, Doctor?" Ambrosini asked Anya.

"Hotel del Sole. Along the Riva degli Schiavoni."

"We have a vaporetto waiting outside, behind the Questura. My men will escort you and provide security until all the members of the conspiracy are arrested."

She nodded and turned to Cal. She reached out and curled her hand around his forearm. He put his hand on hers. Her hand was trembling.

"Help me, Cal." Her voice was barely more than a whisper. She was at the end of her rope. She didn't want medical attention, she wanted him.

Well, she had him.

"I need to be there at the ceremony. I must. My boss, Larry Silver, will be there for the gala, but he won't be there in time for the signing ceremony. I must be there tomorrow. So many people have worked so very hard. I can't let them down. If you're with me, I can rest and feel safe."

Oh yeah. He'd be with her.

He nodded.

Ambrosini accompanied them to the door. He lifted

Anya's hand and bowed over it. "Dr. Voronova we owe you an enormous debt of gratitude. Without your quick intervention, we could be facing a tragedy and an international crisis. We owe you an undying debt of gratitude."

She studied his face. "Find my friend, please. Make sure she is safe."

Cal gently took her phone and held it up to Farris and Ambrosini. "Here's her number, this is what she looks like. Farris, I'm sending you the recording. The woman saved the Accords, let's find her and keep her safe." Farris and Ambrosini were taking note of her number and the recording. He took Anya's arm. "In the meantime, I am taking my woman to her hotel and making sure she sleeps soundly and makes it to the signing ceremony tomorrow." He looked everyone in the eye. "Any objections?"

"We'll stake out the Hotel del Sole, boss. The two of you can sleep easy tonight."

"And my men will form a further security perimeter," Ambrosini said.

Cal nodded. He had no intention of sleeping, but he had every intention of making sure Anya slept.

She was his now, once again, and he was going to take really good care of her. By some miracle, they'd been given a second chance and he was going to grab that with both hands.

11

T he next day was cold, but bright and sunny. Everything gleamed in the vivid light of the hour before sunset. The colors of Venice — red and gold and ochre caught between the blue lagoon and the blue sky — shone and shimmered.

The Venetians knew how to do pageantry right, Anya thought as she looked out over the crowd in St. Mark's Square. Everyone was waving the blue, gold and green flag of the Accords, and everyone was excited.

Nobody knew how close they had come to not having the Accords at all. She couldn't bear to think of the chaos and violence that would have ensued. Centuries of hatred and distrust breaking out again, worse for having had hopes dashed.

But now it was a done deal. At the podium, erected right in front of St. Mark's Cathedral, the very symbol of the marriage of East and West, covered in blue, gold and green bunting, the heads of state of the six signatory guarantor countries had just finished signing the Accords, printed on parchment and bound as a book as thick as the Gutenberg Bible.

The United States, the United Kingdom, Russia, China, France, Saudi Arabia. Forty other countries would sign the Accords after that. The 120 NGOs, including Peace and Jobs, would be signing at the gala dinner and her boss would be here for that. He was in the air right now, his plane about to land.

The final signing was here at last, after which there would officially be peace in a part of the world that had been at war for a millennium. Quite an accomplishment.

As the signing ceremony ended, twenty trumpeters in bright medieval garb, and in the colors of Venice — red and gold — rose, put the long, shiny, medieval trumpets to their mouths and sounded a loud fanfare. A thousand doves were released and rose in the air with a loud flutter.

"Hope they weren't recently fed." Cal bent over and whispered in her ear, with a quick wink.

"Pigeon guano," she whispered back. "A longstanding Venetian tradition."

The fanfare ended, the bright brassy notes lingering in the clear air, so pure you could almost see them shimmering. A conductor in tails stood up, baton in hand, brought his arms up and sharply down, beginning a thrilling rendition of *Sheherezade* from the orchestra seated on the right-hand side of the colorful podium.

Anya and Cal were sitting on bleachers to the left, together with everyone who had worked directly on the Accords. At least two thousand people stood in the piazza to honor the Accords, standing stock still, in utter silence. Many had tears running down their faces.

Anya was too happy to cry, even tears of joy.

Today's ceremony was the culmination of years and years of unremitting effort that was ultimately successful and would change millions of lives for the better.

She was feeling just fine. Last night, Cal had taken her back to her hotel, posted his company's guards on the floor of her hotel room, assuring that there was a second perimeter of Italian police, and guarded her sleep. He'd understood that she was too exhausted and traumatized for sex. He hadn't even mentioned it, though she couldn't help but notice that he'd sported an impressive erection. Not that he'd tried to act on it. Not at all.

He'd gently washed her and put her to bed as tenderly as a mother with her child. And then he'd sat in a chair by her bed, holding her hand. When she woke up in the early afternoon, he was there, clear-eyed, wide awake.

She'd slept deeply, for over twelve hours.

Cal had ordered room service — truffle tagliatelle and a glass of Pinot Grigio, perfection itself — and waited while she dressed. Then they'd walked the short distance to St. Mark's Square along the Riva degli Schiavoni for the late afternoon ceremony.

He'd arranged for her bags to be packed and delivered to his suite at the Hotel Danieli. As if aware of the fact that he was being bossy, he lifted his eyebrows while arranging this with her hotel's concierge and she nodded. It was all okay.

Anya felt strange. Good, but strange. The long and deep sleep, watched over by Cal, had restored her. But she felt light, as if she could float away at any moment. The signing ceremony had freed her, in a way. Like taking ten years to climb Mount Everest, and then you stood on the peak and you were done. Free.

She'd worked so very hard for the Accords, believing in

them with every fiber of her being, putting everything else in her life aside. And now they were signed. There were going to be complex negotiations to iron out the details of the 1,300 page Accords. It was a done deal, but something this complex needed breathing space and dialogue.

Her job was over.

Anya hadn't much looked beyond the completion of the Accords. Her boss had offered her a renewal of her contract but she'd neither accepted nor declined. But now she knew that her job there was done and a new door had opened and she was going to walk through it with Cal.

Her phone pinged. She didn't really want to talk to anyone, but she saw the name on her screen.

"June!" The face on the screen was her friend, smiling and happy. Completely different from the tense, terrified face she'd seen there last night. "You're ok!"

June smiled, her pretty face beaming. "Yes, more than okay. I'm being protected by a SEAL team, my series on the attempted assassination and coup will be on the front page of the New York Times for three days in a row, I've had two offers from publishers for a book and your boyfriend is going to fly me back to New York on a private jet. Not to mention the fact that the Accords will go through. Doesn't get much better than that."

Anya reached out a finger to touch the image of her friend's face. It was just pixels but at that moment, June felt very close. "I'm so glad."

June smiled, showing a dimple. "He's the one, right? The one who broke your heart."

Anya felt Cal shooting her a glance. "No, actually, I broke his. But — it's okay now. It's all good."

"Excellent!" June's smile got even bigger. "Let's have

lunch at the Flowering Lotus soon. When will you be in New York next?"

Good question. Anya lifted her eyebrows, looking at Cal.

He squeezed her arm. "Whenever you want," he said.

"Soon, Junie." Anya turned back to the screen. "I'm so glad you're all right."

"Me, too," June said fervently. "It was touch and go there. I was holed up in the house of a friend but I didn't know if I was putting her in danger and I didn't know if I'd live out the night. It was awful. I don't know who sent in the SEALs here but I am eternally grateful. Talk to you soon. Bye!"

"I think Farris got in touch with someone who got in touch with someone," Cal said. "And I heard that that fucker Ash is in custody, charged with treason. Pity he's not military, I'd love it if he could do time in Leavenworth. But they'll find somewhere suitable for him."

"We're civilized now, but he deserves to be drawn and quartered," Anya said indignantly. That wasn't quite true. She'd seen medieval woodcuttings of the torture and it was horrific. But Ash Morris had had a hand in attempting to scuttle the biggest peace initiative in the history of mankind and had he been successful, hundreds of millions of lives would have been nastier, and crueler and cut short.

Not to mention arranging to have her tortured. There was that, too.

The orchestra finished and the crowd went wild, clapping and whistling and shouting.

A streak of red from the setting sun painted the lagoon crimson.

A soprano came to the podium, a young, pretty Middle Eastern-looking woman with flowing dark hair. The crowd quieted. She touched the microphone as two more doves were set free at her feet. She stood at her ease, a remarkable feat for someone who looked so young. It was a momentous occasion, one that was being filmed by every single TV station on earth, broadcast to over five billion people. And yet she stood quietly, relaxed, a gentle smile on her face.

She sang a cappella in a strong yet delicate voice.

The Long and Winding Road.

There was utter silence in the square as her voice rose, floated above the crowd that had just witnessed history being made. Something textbooks would be analyzing for the next thousand years. Maybe what had happened here today even represented a true turning point in human history. Maybe peace would be forever from now on.

Anything was possible.

Peace and hope were in the air, almost palpable.

Certainly peace and hope and joy were in her heart.

Lead me to your door ...

The door to her heart was wide open.

The last lingering notes of the beautiful song floated in the air. The setting sun burnished the buildings in St. Mark's Square a deep red-gold, a color taken from antiquity.

There was a hushed moment as if the thousands of people in the piazza had been holding their breath, then they broke out in wild applause, echoing off the walls, so loud it must have been heard throughout the city.

Cal grabbed her hand. "Our cue to leave."

"Oh! There are going to be fireworks later. Don't you want to see them?"

"Sure. But my suite looks out over the lagoon. We can watch it from my balcony and sip champagne."

"Being rich does have its advantages," she said drily.

"And thanks for the private jet for June. I think it makes her feel safe."

"That and four SEALs en route with her. Make anyone feel safe."

"Yeah."

In the incredibly crowded square, Cal was managing to steer her through the masses of people with minimum fuss and maximum efficiency. Everyone was happy, everyone was smiling, as they moved and shifted out of their way.

The Hotel Danieli was not far from St. Mark's Square and the streets there weren't crowded. With the setting sun, the colors grew deeper, the city almost impossibly beautiful. Nothing had changed in Venice for centuries. Except for the way she and Cal were dressed, they could have been citizens of La Serenissima from the 17th century out for an evening stroll.

The Hotel Danieli was stunning, the finest hotel in the city, one of the finest in the world. The budget of Peace and Jobs didn't stretch to five star hotels. Her own hotel was nice, but nothing like this.

It looked like something out of the 1001 Nights of Sheherezade that they'd just listened to — sumptuous, marble and teak walls, huge crystal chandeliers, huge, richly decorated vases full of fresh flowers, whose perfume mixed with the perfume of the guests and the brine of the lagoon and the hope in the air.

Cal collected the key at the elaborate, teak front desk. It was an old fashioned, huge, brass key with a dusky pink silk tassel. When he opened the door to his suite and gestured her to enter, she walked in and smiled, bedazzled.

A special place for this special day seemed really right.

The suite was enormous, a living room area, a dining

area and a huge bedroom. Big French windows with gauzy curtains floating in the breeze opened out onto the lagoon, with a waist-high, wrought-iron balcony to keep you from tumbling into the water.

Anya wandered to the windows, still feeling light as the breeze that moved the curtains. Cal stood behind her, big hands heavy on her shoulders. She welcomed that, welcomed his heat, the strong hands grounding her, the feeling of intense connection after years of rootlessness.

The flutter of colors captured her attention. "Oh, look!"

The first ceremonial gondola floated by from St. Mark's Square. Jet black, decorated with bronze dragons, elaborate, red tapestried chairs with gold backs. Four men, two women. The heads of state of the United States, France, the United Kingdom, Russia, Saudi Arabia and ... there he was! The President of China, grinning broadly, waving at the jubilant crowds packed along the square.

Another ceremonial gondola, steered by a handsome gondolier, followed, then another.

"Fifty gondolas," she murmured. "Sailing to the Isola San Giorgio."

"It's official," Cal murmured behind her. "And I am one billion dollars richer."

That surprised a laugh out of her. She turned to look at him and saw, to her surprise, that he was not smiling.

"You're serious?"

He nodded. "Damn right. We worked eighteen-hour days in desert areas, often under siege from hostile tribes, while solving about ten technical impossibilities a day. We're going to provide drinking water for peoples who have never had it. I'm giving a million dollar bonus to every single engineer working for me, and they've earned it."

She blinked at him. "You're — you're richer than my dad ever was?"

"I think so, baby." He grinned and winked at her.

"Huh." Well, that would take some thinking about. Anya stared out at the intensely blue lagoon, the islands like red-gold mirages on the horizon. "Oh, look! That's my boss!"

"Where?" Calvin leaned forward, pressing her against the wrought iron balcony.

"There. In the sixth gondola. The white haired guy in the middle. Larry Silver." She watched fondly as his gondola floated by. If she thought he could see her, she'd have waved, but he was just a little vain and refused to wear his glasses on ceremonial occasions. She knew that the shoreline would be a colorful blur for him. "He made it in time. There's the ceremonial gala dinner tonight on the Isola San Giorgio. Luckily Larry's here so I don't have to attend, not that I would have, anyway." She sighed as he crossed his arms over her waist. "This is much nicer."

"Damn straight." Cal nipped her earlobe, then licked it. He pressed against her and she could feel his erection against the small of her back. "We'll have room service dinner here as soon as we've sorted things out."

Anya thought she knew what he wanted sorted out. Their future. She'd thought they'd talk about it in the coming days but he wanted to talk about it now. He turned her in his arms so she was facing him.

"So what now?" he asked, face somber. Much too somber for such a happy occasion.

"In what way?"

"Where do we go from here? Where do you want to go from here? Do you want to stay on at Peace and Jobs?"

Anya gave a half laugh and with a wave of her arm

took in everything — the lagoon with the parade of gondolas and dignitaries floating by in the golden light of the setting sun, the amazingly beautiful hotel suite, Cal here with her after so many years. "You want to talk about this now?"

"Yes." His features set, sandy eyebrows scrunched together in a scowl, fierce yellow gaze focused like a laser beam on her. "I want to talk about this now. Right now. Are you going to stay on at your old job?"

She sighed. "Well, to tell you the truth, I've been asking myself the same thing. What Peace and Jobs was established to do has been achieved. From now on, I think it'll be more bureaucratic management than anything else. I was thinking of taking some time off and looking around."

He took her chin in his hand, keeping her face still and turned to his. "Don't look any further than me. Phoenix Enterprises is mainly made up of engineers and security guys. The engineers don't know languages or diplomacy. They really don't know anything except numbers and material science and chemistry. And the security guys know close quarter combat and guns. We really need someone like you, someone who will run interference with the million bureaucracies we'll be dealing with. We need to be able to not piss anyone off while doing our job. You'd be absolutely perfect. The company needs you." He swallowed, Adam's apple bobbing. "By God, I need you."

Oh my. Anya ran the back of her fingers down his cheek, his skin warm and just slightly bristly. Suddenly, it was hard to remember that young man so long ago. Who'd been such a tender lover. So very young, just making his way in the world. With no cynicism or calculation in him. What you saw was what you got.

He'd been completely replaced by this powerful man with lines in his face and calluses on his hands.

But he still looked at her the same way.

It all fell into place, with an almost audible click. They were meant to be together *now*. They'd been way too young ten years ago. Her family problems would have snarled him up, her deep desire for adventure and to make a mark in the world would have been unassuaged.

They were right for each other now, with years and miles on them. A long and winding road.

Anya wrapped her arms around his neck, pressing against him, feeling his penis swell. His eyes widened. Her body answered with prickling skin and a flush of heat, warmth between her thighs.

They didn't need words, but she was going to use them anyway. "So ... you're offering me a job?"

"Mm." He held her backside while rolling his hips against hers. "You could say that, yeah. I'd put you in charge of external relations so me and my engineers don't have to do anything but solve technical problems. You can deal with the people problems."

She smiled. "I was paid pretty well at Peace and Jobs. Can you top my salary?"

"Oh, I'll do more than that. I'll double it. Triple it. Quadruple it."

Anya frowned. "You're a terrible negotiator, you do need my help. You shouldn't offer to double or triple or quadruple my salary. Not at the beginning of negotiations. I'll know that I can push you higher."

"You can push me anywhere you want," he said and flashed a wicked grin. Oh man. It was the grin of a powerful man, a predator even. Not her sweet young lover. This was a man who'd created an empire and though his company was brilliant, there was no doubt he'd had to be very tough along the way. Companies like his didn't rise to those heights by playing nice.

She studied his face, all hard planes and weatherbeaten skin. Not the look of a pampered rich man, but definitely the look of a powerful businessman. Also the look of an aroused man. His eyes were narrowed until only the smallest slit of glinting gold showed. His cheeks were red with arousal, his mouth red too with engorged blood. They hadn't kissed yet but he had the look of a man who'd just kissed.

She imagined she had that same look.

They stared into each other's eyes, both aware of the significance of the moment. Both aware that this was a huge turning point for both of them.

"Come with me," Cal whispered. He meant come with me to bed. But he also meant come with me for the rest of my life. For the rest of our lives. He hadn't said the words, but he didn't have to.

Anya answered in the only way she could. "Gladly."

It was like a dream, their movements slow, unhurried. They'd both learned patience over the past ten years. Not one second had been easy, for either one of them. And nobody could know what the future held. The only thing they knew was that they would be facing it together.

Cal kissed her, gently, then hard. But he lifted his mouth, a signal that this time would be gentle and easy. He turned her, unzipped her dress. It was a dress she'd bought in Beirut, pure silk, midnight blue, light as a breeze. She'd bought it for the ceremony but somehow she'd been thinking of Cal when she bought it. It was a color he loved.

"I love this color on you," he murmured as he spread the

wings of the dress. His rough hands smoothed out over her back, pulling the sides of the dress forward. He kissed her back.

Her head hung low. She'd pinned up her hair and he pulled the pins out one by one, spreading her hair out over her shoulders. She smiled secretly. "I know. I remember. I think I was thinking of you when I bought it."

She could feel the breath leaving his body in a whoosh. He spoke with his lips on the skin of her back. "Don't say things like that. Couldn't you have called me, sent up a flare, something?"

Yes. It hurt her heart too to think of all those wasted years. She remembered very clearly buying the dress. She'd represented Peace and Jobs for two and a half months there, holding endless talks with people who hated each other and her. It had been a low point. The city was rebuilding, some crazy people actually believing in peace. But the dust of all the bombed-out buildings was constantly in the air and she'd had a low-grade fever all the time she'd been there.

Going out to buy a pretty dress had been almost an act of defiance. A hope in some nebulous future that would be better than the present.

And she'd thought of Cal as she bunched the beautiful material in her hands, holding it, dreaming of him.

Cal pushed the dress off her and she turned to face him, in only her bra and panties and thigh-high stockings.

She cupped his jaw. "I missed you. I missed you so much, every day it seemed. But when I bought this dress, though lonely and missing you, I was dedicated to the job, a thousand percent. I wanted you but there was no room in my life. And I imagine you were out in the desert then, wrestling with recalcitrant pipelines."

She smiled, reached up to kiss him. "The time is right, *now*. The stars are aligned *now*. And I know I will cherish you all my life because I know how lonely I've been without you. We had to get to this point."

Cal opened his mouth, closed it. "God," he muttered. Her underwear was swept away by some magic wind. His clothes too. And then they were naked together, chest to chest and he was kissing her as if he would die if he didn't.

Oh, yeah. Anya lifted herself up, arms tight around his neck, trying to touch as much of him as she could, because every inch of skin that wasn't touching Cal was dead. His touch was magic, gave life.

He held her tightly and she wrapped her legs around his waist. The tip of his penis brushed her open sex and she moaned.

Yes. Just like that.

Cal held her, entered her and dropped to the bed on top of her, already moving strongly inside her. Anya wrapped her arms and her legs around him, welcoming everything he did. It was all pleasing. He was moving so strongly the head-board beat against the silk covered walls. She hoped that the inhabitants of the room next door were out in the square celebrating what she and Cal had worked so hard and so long for.

But she didn't really care.

Everything spiraled inside her, tighter and tighter and she exploded so hard that it seemed as if it made a noise. Like everyone could hear her climax.

Another *boom* and Cal came inside her, shuddering and shaking. Another boom and she saw red behind her closed eyelids. She sighed as Cal settled heavily on her, then rolled over to the side. She cracked her eyes open and saw — liter-ally — fireworks.

Anya lay, exhausted, Cal curled next to her. Every muscle felt lax and she barely had the energy to keep her eyes open. Another loud *boom!* sounded over again the lagoon.

A starburst of light exploded in the dark night sky, red, gold and green. Then another starburst and another. The opening barrage of the fireworks celebrating the Accords.

She laughed weakly. "It's like a movie soundtrack. How did they know to time it to our orgasms?"

"They have cameras," Cal said seriously. "Our love-making was filmed and projected onto a huge screen in St. Mark's Square."

Anya moved to elbow him in the ribs, but it was a weak effort. "Not funny." Though actually it was.

He turned his head lazily to smile at her. "You realize we haven't used birth control? Not once?"

Anya sighed. "You're right." Her legs moved restlessly and she could feel his semen sticky between her thighs. "We didn't."

Cal shifted a little to look her square in the face. "Doesn't make any difference. We're getting married just as soon as we can."

It wasn't a question.

"Calvin Burns." Anya tried to drum up some indignation. Her first — and presumably only — marriage proposal and he botched it! "That was the worst marriage proposal I've ever heard. You can do better than that."

"Okay." He rolled over in the opposite direction and pulled open the drawer of the ornate bedside table on his side of the bed. Three small boxes dropped on to her naked belly. "I *can* do better." He took her hand in his.

"Anya Voronova, will you do me the honor of becoming my wife?"

Anya didn't even have to think about it. "Yes. Yes, I will. Of course I will. What are these?"

"Open them and see."

Three boxes. "So — three boxes? Three different components of something? Is this some kind of tricky engineering thing I'm going to have to assemble?"

He smiled. Clearly, he wasn't going to answer.

"Okay. Let's see what we have here." She examined the first box, from a local jewelry store. Her heart started thumping. Each box was sumptuously wrapped, with marbleized paper and a big satin bow. She carefully undid the first box, lifted the lid. Lifted the jeweler's box inside the box. It was sumptuous dark blue leather with Bulgari engraved on it.

"Oh." Her breath stopped in her chest as she lifted the lid. It was a ring. A truly glorious ring, a huge, gorgeous sapphire surrounded by pave diamonds. "It's beautiful."

He stopped her hand with his. "There's a choice. Open the other two as well."

She looked at him curiously then opened the next box. Another amazing sapphire, a cabochon set, a more modern design.

He nudged her with his shoulder. "Open the last one."

Smiling, she did. Yet another sapphire set in diamonds with a platinum band this time. A Bulgari Trombino. They were all famous Bulgari designs.

The rings were lying on the flat of her palm. "Cal, I don't know which one to choose. They're all so beautiful. I can't believe you remembered that my favorite stone is sapphire."

His eyes were serious as they looked into hers. "Your birth stone. I could never forget."

She stared at the three gorgeous rings in her hand, trying to pick a favorite.

He closed her hand around them. "And I don't want you to choose. All three are yours. All you have to choose is which one will be your engagement ring."

Anya stared at him. "When did you have time to go out and buy rings?"

"You forget." Cal's mouth lifted in a half smile. "I'm an engineer. A problem solver. I went to the Bulgari website because I remembered that you dragged me to that jewelry show when we were kids and you oohed and aahed over the Bulgari jewelry. I thought that if I ever became rich, I'd buy you Bulgari jewelry. So I narrowed it down to three, clicked on the images, got in touch with the Bulgari shop here and had them send all three over to the Danieli." He lifted a broad shoulder. "Problem solved."

Anya clenched her hand around the three rings. She'd cherish them all her life.

"They come with a price," Cal warned.

"Yeah?"

"Yeah. Marriage just as soon as we can arrange it, here in Venice if we can, tomorrow if we can. And I want kids."

"Kids plural?"

"Kids plural." He poked her belly gently with a finger. "And I want a girl."

Anya sighed, completely happy. "Well, I'll do my best. And do you know what we'll call her?"

He smiled into her eyes. "Gondola?"

She laughed and backhanded his chest.

"No, silly. Venetia."

PREVIEWS

Dear Reader, I hope you enjoyed **MASQUERADE Her Billionaire – Venice.** If you did, I'd appreciate a review.

You might also enjoy **CHARADE Her Billionaire – Paris** and **ESCAPADE Her Billionaire – London,** two more sexy, sophisticated stories. Here are the first chapters of CHARADE and ESCAPADE:

1

CHARADE PREVIEW
THE RITZ, PARIS

"More wine?" Mark Redmond asked, hand around the neck of a bottle of *Châteauneuf-du-Pape*. Beneath his stylish and very expensive suit, he was at heart a barbarian, but even he knew it was an excellent wine.

He watched as Harper Kendall, the most enticing woman he'd ever met, pondered his question.

He could almost see the wheels turning in her beautiful head. It really was a good wine and she'd only had one glass to his three. But—was he trying to get her drunk? Trying to seduce her?

No. And yes.

God yes, he was trying to seduce her. He'd been thinking about getting her into his bed since he'd first set eyes on her on the business-class trip from Boston to Paris.

His company had two corporate jets but he had two teams he was sending into failed states and harm's way. He wanted them to get there rested and refreshed, so he had them use the Falcon 8X and the Gulfstream G3.

Going to Paris for a few days before his meeting with the

head of a big bank had been a last-minute decision; he hadn't had time off since forever. First class had been fully booked and he'd been amused when he'd caught himself thinking that he'd have to 'settle' for business class. Especially considering how, in his military days, he'd crisscrossed the world in noisy, cold C-130s strapped to the bulkhead, pissing in a bottle.

In the end, going business class was the best thing to happen to him in a long, long time, when he'd seen the beauty sitting in the seat next to his.

"Sure," she said and nudged her glass closer to him. Mark filled the big balloon glass one third full, the canonical amount. Any less and it would have seemed stingy. Any more and she would have reason to suspect he was trying to get her drunk.

He didn't want her drunk, but he did want her happy.

Being with a woman like Harper was challenging, full of hidden pitfalls. Good thing he was a man who relished challenges.

She sipped, watched him a bit warily over the rim of her crystal goblet. "So, do you know Paris well?"

"Been here a few times but always briefly, for work. In and out."

Her lips curled in a smile. "Plumbing supply imports."

"That's right." Mark leaned back and watched her. He always chose the most boring jobs possible for cover. Plumbing supply importer, accountant, tax software salesman. "Fly in, make a deal, fly out. This time I wanted to take a day or two to sightsee. Do you know Paris well?"

"Yes, I do." She took another sip. "I studied French here for a summer, just out of high school, then came for a semester during my master's. I love this city."

There. An opening. Mark waited for her to offer to show him around Paris. But...crickets. He stifled a sigh. Still, he was a man who knew how to make his own opportunities.

"Maybe some other evening you'd have dinner with me. After work. You're here for research, right?"

"Mmm." She smiled. "Some business and some research."

"For that book?" His gorgeous princess had written and published one book and was writing her second, which he really admired. Mark couldn't write a book to save his life. He could kill a man at a thousand yards, but he couldn't write a book.

The smile grew. "That's right. Linking historical political movements to architectural styles. I'm keeping it accessible though, not a cultural tract. Are you interested in architecture, Mark?"

He sat back. "I can't say I'm particularly knowledgeable about architecture and its history. I'll happily read your first book, though. It sounds really interesting."

"Well, that's kind. You don't have to do that."

"I want to." And he did.

"I'll write down the title for you."

He deliberately didn't smile. "The title has three words in it. I think can remember them. So—how about dinner tomorrow evening?"

She didn't answer, just looked at him. Mark understood exactly what was happening. She was consulting her internal self on whether she wanted a second date and the only intel she had on him was what he was giving her. He couldn't tell her who he really was, but he could give her his essence.

He was a good guy. He wasn't going to hurt her. He

wanted sex with her badly, more than any woman he could ever remember, but it had to be mutual and he'd treat her well.

He couldn't say that in words but he could show her via his body language. So he sat very, very still, and watched her face. He was probably emitting pheromones by the ton because she was just so goddamn luscious, and he'd had a semi hard-on all through dinner, but that was okay. She had to know he desired her. They'd been in constant contact since they'd first boarded that flight and though he'd been respectful, he'd also made it clear that he was attracted.

Putting it mildly.

She was, too. This was a strong-minded woman and she wouldn't be sitting here having dinner with him at the Ritz if she didn't want to be.

She sighed. "Dinner tomorrow evening? I don't know when I'll finish up with my work."

"Doesn't make any difference," he answered. "I don't have a timetable. I came in early to rest and to sightsee a little." He shrugged. "I've been working really hard lately, and I decided to just relax for a day or two. So I can work around your schedule, no problem."

Harper made a little humming sound, as if thinking over reasons to say no. But she really wanted to say yes. She was a real beauty, so she'd probably spent half her life saying no to men, decisively. She wouldn't be humming if it was a decisive "no".

She looked at their table, at the remains of an excellent meal, at the elegant room. Everyone dressed up, the waiters the most elegant of all, low voices, the gleaming crystal glasses, the chandeliers like crystal clouds, everyone smiling in their comfortable upholstered settees.

It was a feast for all the senses.

"Okay, but not at the Ritz. And it's on me next time."

"Not a chance, but nice try," Mark said. "And we can go anywhere you want. I'm not fussy."

He wasn't. He'd once lived for three weeks on MREs— gummy tubes of nutrients that tasted like cardboard, no matter what the label said. He hadn't liked it but he'd done it.

"We'll see then. Do you want to enter my cell number in your cell?"

"No need." He rattled off her ten-digit number. "You gave me your card on the plane, remember?"

She blinked. "Wow. You have quite a memory if you remember it from my business card."

He shrugged. "I'm good with numbers. My business is figures on spreadsheets. A little less interesting than your business."

She smiled. "I love what I do. So, what do you know about architecture?"

"Not much." He knew nothing about architecture, but he did know a lot about buildings. Particularly how to blow them up. "But I'd love to learn."

She looked around. "This building, for example. The façade dates back to the early eighteenth century and it's part of the seamless Place Vendôme. It's said that this hotel was the first in the world to offer en-suite bathrooms."

He shook his head. "About the only thing I know about its history is that Hemingway 'liberated' the Ritz bar in 1944, gulping down its best wine that they'd hidden from the Nazis, while snipers were still shooting on the outskirts of Paris."

Harper put back her head and laughed, and all Mark could do was stare at her.

In the fanciest restaurant in Paris, possibly in the world, Harper Kendall was the classiest, most beautiful woman there. He watched as she tipped her head back slightly, exposing that long, slim neck, and gave a genuine laugh. It wasn't meant to entice him, she was genuinely amused. But God, she enticed him.

Tilting her head made that shiny mass cascade over her shoulders. Those light gray cat's eyes narrowed as she laughed and she simply took his breathe away.

Though Mark was used to hiding his feelings, something of what was going on inside of him—maybe a sudden surge of testosterone—made her still and look at him, startled and then wary.

One of the many waiters started walking toward them with the dessert menu in his hand. Mark caught his eye and made a subtle gesture with his hand.

Not now.

You didn't get to be a waiter at the Ritz by being a fool. A simple nod of the head and the waiter faded away.

Mark had other plans for dessert.

He leaned forward slowly. "I know it sounds pedestrian, but I'd really like a Crêpe Suzette for dessert. How about you?"

He kept his voice even, trying to keep himself under control.

"Crêpes Suzette wasn't on the dessert menu. There was pineapple ravioli with wasabi yogurt sauce and Bresse cheese with red onion marmalade." She smiled at him. "I have a good memory too, just not for numbers."

"No, I meant Crêpes Suzette somewhere else. My room,

here at the Ritz." Mark covered her slender hand with his. She was acting cool, but her hand was trembling slightly. "It's on the room service menu. And we could pair it with some more champagne or some Grand Marnier."

She looked at him, her luscious mouth slightly open. Silvery-gray eyes wary.

He waited.

She wasn't saying no.

She wasn't saying yes, either.

He kept his hand over hers. It was warm and soft, fingers long and elegant.

Mark's voice was low, without urgency, though desire prickled through his veins. "I have a suite. We could sit and talk in private." He looked around the beautiful room, full of customers. "Where no one could bother us."

He tightened his hold on her hand, but just slightly. He had big strong hands and he didn't want to hurt her or make her feel coerced. She watched him silently, hand still slightly trembling under his.

"I promise you that nothing will happen that you don't want to happen. If all you want is a Crêpe Suzette and a glass of champagne or Grand Marnier and a chat, that's fine. I'll take it and I'll be happy. But I won't hide from you that I'd like more."

She still didn't say anything. Just sat there, eyes looking into his, darting back and forth, making little silver flashes like lightning.

"Your call." Then Mark shut up.

Maybe more words would convince her. She was a writer, eloquent words probably mattered to her. But he didn't have eloquence in him. He was a straightforward kind of guy. He'd said what he needed to say. He'd told her he wanted her. If he elaborated on that, said that he was burning up with desire, that he wanted her like he wanted his next breath, he might scare her away.

Also, he'd made it clear that she could trust him. And she could, even if it killed him.

He waited to see what she would say. He couldn't remember wanting anything more than he wanted her. Like the song said, every move she made fascinated him. His entire body was tense, waiting for her response. He was tense between his legs, too. He had to will the hard-on down by thinking of Afghanistan, thinking of the men who died or were maimed there.

It was hard though. Afghanistan was now seven thousand miles and years away but Harper was right here, right now. She was a stunner with light brown hair that turned silver in the light, matching her silvery-gray eyes with a dark blue rim. They nearly glowed in the dark. She had a heart-shaped face with silky-smooth pale skin and a mouth that was made for kissing. All this paired with small, perfect breasts, a tiny waist and long legs.

But more than that she was smart, with a dry sense of humor and a bottomless fund of knowledge of the world. He'd never met anyone quite like her, and he wanted her so much it made his hands itch and his dick twitch.

He wanted to make love to her, but it had to be mutual. She had to want it too. He'd rather tear out his own throat than hurt her or force her.

She still didn't say anything, but he could see her rolling the idea around in that beautiful head of hers. That was okay. He was a patient man. He could wait. And for her? For her, he'd wait a long, long time.

Now that she was in his head, he couldn't even imagine

desiring someone else. She was everything he could possibly want in a woman. Smart, classy, gorgeous.

She waited for a beat. Two.

Then she twisted her hand under his.

For a horrific moment, Mark thought she was going to pull her hand away, get up and walk out.

But no.

Her palm came to rest against his palm and her fingers clasped his.

His heart gave a sharp thump in his chest.

It was a yes.

2

ESCAPADE PREVIEW

CALVIN BYRNES BUILDING,
MATHEMATICAL INSTITUTE

OXFORD

S he was a looker.

Really gorgeous in a punk schoolmarm-y kind of way. Not that any of the males in the room would notice. There was very little testosterone in this room of two hundred math geeks, most of them guys. More or less all the testosterone in the room was his, and it was sitting up and taking notice.

Not good.

Bennett Cameron wasn't used to having testosterone released during a job for anything but aggression. He was a close protection expert — a bodyguard, in civilian terms — and he was used to being alert to anything that could be a source of danger. When on the clock, his body was flooded with testosterone and cortisol, the arousal and stress hormones. Arousal as in all systems go, every sense up and running, including the sixth one.

Not arousal as in a hard-on.

He'd been a security consultant long enough to have a sixth and even seventh sense for danger. Nothing got by him.

Right now, nothing was pinging on his danger radar so all that testosterone went to one special part of his body, watching the lithe young beauty parade across the stage, mouthing mathematical formulae, following abstruse lines of thought, of which he understood one word in ten.

Still, he didn't have to understand her math. He just had to keep her safe.

But first he had to kidnap her.

That was a royal pain in the ass. And maybe not easy, either. Bennett watched her on the stage, pacing back and forth, elaborating some incredibly long and complicated thought that had the audience gasping, then tittering, then sighing. Whatever she was saying — and he had no hope of deciphering it — was a real hit with the geeks.

But where the geeks and nerds all looked lost, with their too big sweaters that looked like their moms had dressed them in expectation of that last spurt of growth, cumulatively smelling a bit rank, completely engrossed in what she was saying, the woman herself, Dr. Eleonore Castle, known by her peers as E. M. Castle for Eleonore Marion Castle, known by her friends as Elle, seemed very alert. Very aware of her surroundings. Those cobalt-blue eyes as she looked around the room seemed very very sharp.

She looked pretty unkidappable if he wanted to keep it calm and quiet.

He was at the back of the room, hiding behind a pillar. The stage lights were in her eyes. There was no chance that she could see him, but still he stuck to the shadows, biding his time. There was no way he could abduct her in front of two hundred geeks.

Well actually he *could* ... given the fitness level of the audience. But they would all surely have cellphones and a robust virtual life more interesting than their real lives, so the scene of Dr. Eleonore Castle being abducted in the civilized confines of the Mathematical Institute of Oxford University would explode and go viral on all social media in about five seconds.

Bennett's company operated below the radar, which is why it was so successful. A media frenzy would be bad for this op in particular and terrible for his company in general. Not to mention it would paint a huge bullseye on the good doctor's very pretty back, when he'd signed a million-dollar contract to protect that back. And front, for that matter.

Her talk was a long one but fascinating, to judge by the rapt expressions of the audience. Bennett himself didn't have a clue.

"And then one could just camp out on the x axis forever, am I right?" she said, bafflingly, and even more bafflingly, the whole room erupted in chuckles.

Well, he wasn't going to kidnap her in the auditorium, and what she was saying was nonsense to him, so he had best use the time in research. He was as good at research as he was in Close Quarters Combat and Close Protection, which was why his company had taken off.

Okay. Nothing like St. Google to give you info and ... oh wow. Pages and pages and *pages* of stuff on Dr. Castle. If you googled his name, Bennett Cameron, you'd get a few very spare returns and a tripwire in one of his back offices would send him a message that someone had pinged him. Bennett operated way under the radar.

But the people with the money to afford him knew about him and knew how to get in touch with him.

So, the very pretty doctor had academic credentials as long as his dick. A doctorate and two masters and a number of seminars that she both attended and taught. A list of publications that was impressive for someone so young, including two books. Wait — he didn't know how old she was. Her father hadn't told him. And she looked really young up there on the stage. And she had a doctorate and two masters and all those courses, so how the hell —

Oh. She went to Harvard when she was fourteen.

Damn.

A lot of brain power in that pretty head.

Bennett looked at what she'd been doing the past six months. Most people were creatures of habit and if you wanted to know where they were and what they were doing, your best bet was to check where they'd been and what they'd done.

Conferences all over the place, with strange names. Behavioral Economics, Mechanism Design, Circuits and Systems. Conferences in Berkley, Singapore, St. Petersburg, Las Vegas, Guangzhu, Abu Dhabi, just in the last six months alone. The woman got around.

This was not a bad thing. He could pass for a math nerd for about ten seconds and say they'd met at a conference. She couldn't possibly remember everyone she met when she was on the road so much.

So that was the play.

Catch her after the symposium, tell her they'd met in wherever, whenever, get her in a quiet space, explain about her father, whisk her away.

Done deal.

So Bennett waited patiently for her to finish her incomprehensible talk and tried not to let his mind wander. Someone in close protection never let their mind wander, ever. Intense vigilance while on the job was a prerequisite. Lose focus for a second and you could lose a life.

But right now, there was nothing to do and there was no imminent danger so he could relax his vigilance, just a bit.

He had a perfect view of the main entrance to the auditorium. There was a small hidden door behind the podium, too. Nobody could come in without him seeing who it was. If anything happened in the auditorium itself, if anyone stood up to shoot her, Bennett would shoot him first. He and his company worked often for the UK government and he had been granted a license to carry in the UK. He was an excellent shot. A former sniper, in fact.

So Bennett kept an eye on the beauty up on stage with a part of his head thinking in non-tactical terms.

Slender, long-limbed, agile. She paced gracefully as she unwound a long, involved line of reasoning that took up three slides of dense math on the screen. Bennett lost track immediately.

Man, she was just amazing. Particularly considering that her father, Clifford Ricks, resembled a toad. Eleonore or Elle or Ellie was the man's only child, fruit of his first marriage. The old man had gone on to five more marriages, each divorce costing him more than ten million dollars. Luckily, he had money to spare.

She was wearing a jacket that could only be described as post-modern. Cut askew, it was both weird and attractive because it hugged her slender curvy figure and it was a deep brilliant cobalt blue that exactly matched her eyes. And she was wearing tight, stovepipe black pants that exactly matched the color of her hair.

Bennett didn't often get a chance to admire who he was protecting, not in this way. He'd protected beautiful women before, usually the wives of rich men, their minds as empty as their faces were beautiful. Though, to tell the truth, he didn't do much close protection himself these days. He had men for that. A hundred and fifty of them, to be exact, all of them hand-picked.

It was a young man's game and though Bennett wasn't old, he wasn't young any more either. Too old for this kind of work. His company was moving into more intel-dense work, finding missing people, tracking down money launderers, that kind of thing.

He'd only accepted this contract because Clifford Ricks had begged him. Saying he'd get on his knees if he still could. Ricks's hedge fund had thrown millions of dollars' worth of work to Bennett's company and, well, a young woman in danger. It wasn't in him to refuse.

And now that he'd had a glimpse of the daughter, he was more glad than ever that he'd accepted the job.

Clifford Ricks's enemy was Anton Lipov, who headed an offshoot of the Volcic mob, known for its extreme cruelty. They placed their enemies on a meat hook and watched them die, over the course of days.

That wasn't going to happen to Elle Castle.

Whoa. The talk was over. Elle took a little sardonic bow as the auditorium rose, clapping.

Fuck. They all looked eager to rush to the podium to grab a bite of the star. Bennett couldn't protect her in a crowd, not without showing his hand and it was too early for that. He moved forward, running through scenarios in his head, when she suddenly ... disappeared.

What the hell?

The hidden door behind the podium clicked shut. She'd escaped out the back of the stage. Well, Bennett couldn't fault her. The smell of unwashed clothes and a few whiffs of major halitosis were detectable even at the back of the auditorium. He could only imagine how repulsive the nerds would be up close and personal. But now he was going to have to be fast to catch up with her.

He knew how to move fast without appearing to rush. He had long legs and he lengthened his stride without moving his upper body much. In a few seconds he was out the door and into the big hallway. The original building was ancient. He had no idea how ancient but it boasted spires and and flagstoned floors and stained glass windows. The math annexe was modern, though, with acres of carpeted hallways.

Bennett quartered the area without swiveling his head, without making it obvious he was looking for someone. There were three directions she could have gone and he studied each one carefully.

There! Making her way down the hallway which was the fastest route out of the building. And man, she was making tracks.

Bennett lengthened his stride even more. "Elle! Ellie! *Elle Castle*!" he called out behind her, relieved when she slowed and turned around.

"Hey!" Bennett put on his genial good guy face. He'd trained to kill since he was eighteen and he'd killed twelve men in battle and three in close protection. When he wanted to, he could switch to his war face and it was frightening. But he could also smile and look as harmless as someone built like him could look. He pasted a delighted smile on his face. "Good to see you! That was a really interesting talk back there."

Bennett wasn't a ladies' man, but he also wasn't bad

looking and he knew how to charm the ladies when he had to. But Elle wasn't having it and was definitely not charmed. She stared up at him and it was like being caught in the beam of twin cobalt spotlights.

"Do I know you?" she asked, voice cold.

He plastered a hand over his heart. "You wound me, you really do. We shared a glass of indifferent champagne at the reception in St Petersburg. The caviar was good, though."

Her eyes searched his face. "No," she said flatly, "we didn't. I've never seen you before in my life."

Oh man. God save him from smart women with steel trap memories. She also seemed pretty impervious to his charms. Bennett took her arm gently, hoping to walk her closer to the exit door while trying to convince her they'd met before. He remembered the name of one of the authors of a paper.

"Surely you haven't forgotten Leontov too? And his dandruff?" Since the guy was a mathematician, it was a pretty good guess that he had dandruff. Unless he was completely bald. It was a 50-50 shot.

Eleonore Castle dug in her heels. To move her now he'd have to use at least a minimum amount of force. And she'd probably raise a fuss. They were surrounded by people. She looked pointedly at his hand on her elbow. "I'll thank you to stop manhandling me and to leave me alone, otherwise I'm calling security."

Well, she could hardly know that he'd easily deal with a Brit rent-a-cop. Or even several of them.

But they were wasting time on a very time-sensitive mission. Bennett stifled a sigh. He looked down into her beautiful angry mistrustful face and took an executive decision.

"Sorry, darling," he murmured. "I really don't want to do this, but I have to."

And he injected her with a fast-acting psychotropic drug that would make her amenable but not unconscious. She gave a small cry at the slight sting of the needle then, after a moment, her eyes unfocused.

Bennett waited a few seconds for the drug to take effect. He wasn't happy about it. He was a good guy and he was saving her life but man, he didn't like drugging a woman. But she was too smart for her own good, so what choice did he have?

"Come on, darling," he said and took her arm again.

She shambled forward obediently.

ALSO BY LISA MARIE RICE

Black Inc.

Jacob

Nikolai

Ghost Ops

Heart of Danger

I Dream of Danger

Breaking Danger

Men Of Midnight Series

Midnight Man

Midnight Run

Midnight Angel

Midnight Shadows

Midnight Quest

Midnight Fever

Midnight Renegade

Midnight Vengeance

Midnight Promises

Midnight Secrets

Midnight Fire

Women of Midnight

Midnight Kiss

Midnight Embrace

Midnight Caress

Her Billionaire Series

Charade

Masquerade

Escapade

Dangerous Passions

Reckless Night

Hot Secrets

Dangerous

Dangerous Lover

Dangerous Passion

Dangerous Secrets

Small Town Romance

Don't Think Twice

Woman on the Run

A Fine Specimen

The Defenders

Protector

Maverick

Fatal Heat

Taken

Runaway

ABOUT THE AUTHOR

Lisa Marie Rice is eternally 30 years old and will never age. She is tall and willowy and beautiful. Men drop at her feet like ripe pears. She has won every major book prize in the world. She is a black belt with advanced degrees in archaeology, nuclear physics, and Tibetan literature. She is a concert pianist. Did I mention her Nobel Prize?

Of course, Lisa Marie Rice is a virtual woman and exists only at the keyboard when writing romantic suspense. She disappears when the monitor winks off.

OLIVERHEBERBOOKS

A small press bound by the belief that every voice matters.

Sign up for our newsletter to learn about new releases and more.
https://oliver-heberbooks.com/subscribe/

Follow us on social media:

facebook.com/oliverheberbooks

instagram.com/oliverheberbooks

amazon.com/oliverheberbooks

youtube.com/@OliverHeberBooksPublisher